QUINN

EM STRANG

ONEWORLD

A Oneworld Book

First published by Oneworld Publications, 2023

Copyright © Emma Strang 2023
Illustrations © Izzy Williamson 2023

The moral right of Emma Strang to be identified as the
Author of this work has been asserted by her in accordance
with the Copyright, Designs and Patents Act 1988

ISBN 978-0-86154-300-7
eISBN 978-0-86154-301-4

Typeset by Tetragon, London
Printed and bound in Great Britain by Clays Ltd, Elcograf S.p.A.

Oneworld Publications
10 Bloomsbury Street
London WC1B 3SR
England

Stay up to date with the latest books,
special offers, and exclusive content from
Oneworld with our newsletter

Sign up on our website
oneworld-publications.com

MIX
Paper from
responsible sources
FSC® C018072

To Mary

Men have hitherto treated women like birds which have strayed down to them from the heights: as something more delicate, more fragile, more savage, stranger, sweeter, soulful — but as something which has to be caged up so that it shall not fly away.

FRIEDRICH NIETZSCHE

Not everything that is faced can be changed; but nothing can be changed until it is faced.

JAMES BALDWIN

PART I

The sound of a woman praying

1

Things have been done that hurt the mouth to speak of.

Let it be known that I have suffered. I was familiar with suffering in the way only some men are – it was in my blood. It was as though my ancestors had passed suffering on as a gift. A gift in dark blue, almost black wrapping paper that smelt of tar.

Whenever I awoke there was a pressing on my windpipe and a constriction of the space between my ribs and my lungs. I could only speak in a hoarse whisper of how much suffering had come.

I did not ask for pity. I was alive and sometimes I sang or roared the story of my suffering. I knew very little in those days. Perhaps the only thing that was clear to me was that I had to find Andrea, to be reunited with the woman I had lost. I missed her soft voice. I missed the way we would lie together, hands and feet barely touching, like a god and his goddess depicted on an alabaster tomb.

She was a good goddess – we used to joke about this stupid phrase – with a small nose, like a child's button nose, and thin, shoulder-length hair like her mother's; so fine was her hair that it seemed to float around her head like a golden halo. She never fussed about her hair like other women do. It was just hair, in the way breath was breath and flesh, flesh.

I had to search for Andrea, not least because I was the only person who knew where to look. It was obvious that so much of this suffering could have been avoided if they had made an effort to unpick the endless stream of hysterical stories that had been woven around her disappearance.

But it was not to be. Instead, I found myself in a dank little room, with no memory of having got there. I had crossed no roads, waded no river. I had not walked thrice around the rowan tree. When I looked up at the slit – it could not be called a window – I saw the occasional blackbird or seagull in flight. The slit was too high to see through at eye level, even if I stood on an item of furniture, so I had no idea what was nearby. I had no idea where I was. Sometimes I heard doors banging and people's voices – a world of sorts. But I was not alone: grey concrete walls, bed, desk, chair, bucket, slit.

I knew Andrea was in the woods, and I could smell her. She had a sweet, musty smell, the way carnations smell when they start to die. I liked that smell. Perhaps I liked it because it was familiar and I knew the woman it belonged to.

We had loved each other all our lives – since we were five or six years old. No, we had imitated love, pretended love, failed and misunderstood love. Or I had. Andrea understood these things better than I. It is a bitter truth I return to at times of darkness and hopelessness, of which there are many.

It is true that when I speak, I begin to remember. Or when I remember, I begin to speak. It is a difficult process and a long story. Sometimes I prefer watching the sunlight move across the floor. Silence has been a good friend to me over the years, though not in a religious, prayerful way; not in the way my mother would have liked.

Andrea was used to giving up her life for another, to care for and make room for the beating heart of another human being. She knew how to put herself aside without extinguishing herself altogether. She had this fire in her, something I could not touch.

Her fire used to shake me out of my torpor. It was as though this word had come alive inside my heart and inside my gut. Torpor overtook me as if it were a living being, some entity that wished to empty me of all light, all gladness. As a child, I had been able to look at a horse and know gladness deep inside me. Something about the shape and the breath and the presence of the animal told me that life was good, that my body was worthy, that my heart was beating for a reason. But later, this gladness left me and was replaced with torpor, and Andrea was the only person who was able to shake me momentarily free of it. Horses can still bring me back to myself, but there are no horses here.

It was my mother who said to me, 'The horse mocks at fear and is not frightened,' and it was the only time I felt understood by her. It was probably the only time she had *tried* to understand me. She knew that I stopped by the horses on the way home from school all those years, and so she knew that they were a comfort to me. Still, those were words from the Bible; they were not hers.

It is true that I could smell Andrea all the way from this dank, inhospitable room that stifled me. I could smell her over and above the stench of my own excrement in the tin bucket. It was only a matter of time before the door would swing open and I would walk out again to find her.

And when I found her, they would have to eat their words.

2

It was early because the light was only just coming in through the slit and I was drifting in and out of sleep. I heard no knock and the door opened on its own, with no need to unlock or push, even though it was a heavy iron door with hinges the size of crowbars. A man who introduced himself as Martin – his name tag read 'M. Payne' – appeared at the door and led me down a series of corridors to a basement. Everything was painted white, with a faint smell of fresh paint, and there were four doors, all of them dark blue, almost black. Martin stood for a while as though he could not decide which door to open, then he hurried me outside.

The woods were darker than I remembered and dense. Daylight had not yet fully penetrated the crisscross of branches and the place felt inert, more plantation than woodland. Birds were calling – tits, wood pigeons – and everything was wet from recent rain.

As I stepped forwards, mud and leaves reluctantly let go of my boots. There was something erotic about it.

I understood about mud and reluctance and rain.

I headed straight for the silver birch, our tree. The sun was beginning to shine between clouds, and the bark glowed. One white incisor in a forest of teeth – that's what Andrea called it. She was bound to be somewhere near here. This was where we met on Fridays, after she had finished with her mother and I had completed the week's story. A single silver birch in the middle of larch and pine, and the big car-wash brushes of spruce.

The stories I wrote were a waste of time. Nobody understood them. I wanted to say something new and present readers with a challenge, but if I wanted publication, I had to churn out a series of stock images and ideas that people could take comfort from or use to explain the world away. The only acceptance for publication I received was from some marginal magazine called *SeaGlass* and the local *Courier*, where the guidelines for publication were prescriptive and anodyne. I never liked the published stories, but I refused to give up.

There was one story that always stayed with me, though it was never accepted for publication – the one about a woman who turned into a swan. Perhaps it was the transformation motif that appealed to me. The woman was not pure and graceful in the way swans are often symbolised. She was manipulative and controlling and made her lover's life a living hell. I read it to Andrea one afternoon, but she did not like it. It bored her, she said.

I still do not know why, but swans have been an almost constant presence in my life. I could not get away from them even if I had wanted to. Every year I would hear the arrival of the whooper swans, flapping and calling as they flew above our house. They migrated from the north to overwinter on the lake in the local park. My mother would take me to see them, and when I was old enough to go on my own, I would walk the four miles from our house to the park, scuffing and sliding on the icy pavements.

There were the swans, magnificent on the lake, noble, if that is even a word these days. There were always one or two young children with their mothers, but I was the only boy my age to stand at the shore and watch the big birds. I pretended not to care what others thought of me, but I pulled my hat down and wore my scarf over my face.

The swans moved across the water completely. That is why I liked to watch them. They possessed something that I did not, but it has taken me a lifetime to work out what that was, and even now I am not quite sure I have understood.

But I am getting ahead of myself.

One strange year, a pen built her nest in our back garden, beneath the laburnum tree. She laid one egg but it never hatched, and as winter turned to spring, she abandoned the nest and flew away. My father had wanted to kill the bird and roast her, but even he was restrained by the community's interest. It was a rare time of social interaction and friendliness in our street. Neighbours we scarcely knew came to coo over the bird, and my mother would stand proudly, as though the pen were her own child. Mama liked to be the centre of a good story and the swan had chosen *her* back garden, *her* laburnum tree to nest beneath. Surely this was a good sign from God? But something was wrong: swans do not nest and lay eggs in the winter. Our pen was confused, out of sync with the world, or perhaps she was unwell.

The sketches I made and the words I wrote in my journal that winter have stayed with me. I used to sit on my brother's bed as he coughed and wheezed, and read him excerpts: 'The swan is desperate on the nest.'

I had wanted to keep the egg, but my father would not let me. Instead, I was allowed to collect up her stray feathers, and I put them in a jam jar in my bedroom. They were very white. I had hoped for a wing feather, but all she had shed were semi-plumes and contour feathers and down. They shone in the gloom of summer evenings before sleep. Sometimes I imagined they had a life of their own. I often dreamt that they had returned to the body of the pen and that when I woke in the morning, they would no longer be there. But they were always there, until my mother threw them away and recycled the glass jar.

I do not know what happened to the egg. I suspect my father ate it, but I do not know for certain. What is more slippery – a raw swan egg or a father's anger?

As a child, I was thrilled by the swans, and even now they drift into my conscious mind unbidden, as though they are bringing some truth to me. My mother always told me that in Christian narratives the swan symbolised grace and transformation and that if you saw a swan, it was a reminder of the possibility that people too could change for the better.

I had known since before I could walk that laburnum trees were poisonous.

3

Even though the sun was rising fast, it was not easy seeing through the undergrowth. It was not my fault that I had not found Andrea yet. I was dodging branches and brambles. I was doing my best.

They could talk and laugh as much as they liked, but the job of searching was mine. I had to find her and bring her home, and when I did she would thank me. She would take off her coat and kiss me on the lips. Her eyes would shine, up close, and I would feel the movement of her breasts as she breathed in and out alongside me. I had to find her and bring her home, and when I did they would let me be.

It was as though the sun were lying or somehow tricking me. Its bright light was coming down, but it had started to rain. It was not light summer rain, but rain like stair rods, as Andrea's mother would have said. It lashed my scalp and I had to put on my cap and zip up my coat. My coat felt odd, as if it were not mine. The fabric was too coarse for a coat – it was like rough, hairy skin and as the rain beat down, it became slippery.

I walked around the birch tree three times and saw that there was something flapping high up on the trunk. At first I thought it was a leaf, but as I peered through the rain I could make out a paper envelope stuck to the tree high above my head. I stretched up but could not reach it, even on tiptoe with my arm fully out. I kicked about in the undergrowth for a log or some rubbish to stand on – there were often plastic crates dumped here or empty oil cans. I only needed something to lift me about a head and a neck. I went down on my hands and knees to rummage, but all I found was a rusty knife with a bone handle and a snapped-off tip, and a crisp packet that smelt as though it had something disgusting inside.

Repulsive as it was, the crisp packet made me feel hungry and my stomach began to growl. It was the familiar, bright, shiny packet that in previous days had always promised food.

There was nothing edible in my coat pocket, only the small plastic doll that Andrea had bought in Spain. She called it a 'figurine', as though she was trying to impress me with her vocabulary. Of course, I was the writer, not her; I knew about language and its weight, not her. The doll was brightly coloured, almost fluorescent, and it gleamed in the rain-light under the trees. Andrea said she thought it looked like her, that in giving it to me, she would be forever by my side. Something sentimental like that.

I was starving.

There was nothing to stand on, nothing big enough to lift me to the envelope, and the weariness was coming on. My body felt limp and hopeless, and my back was beginning to ache. I lay down in the wet mud, not caring, feeling the rain pelt my body and stream off my face.

The waves of weariness had come, and everything I was doing – the searching – seemed pointless. The paper envelope was flapping on the trunk like a huge moth. I hated moths.

I was going to lie for a long time.

Lying flat on the earth felt good. It made my bones feel solid, real, in a way they never did when I was upright. Andrea understood and often just talking to her about my back eased the pain. She did not think I was making it up. Andrea was beautiful like that. She listened. She had nice skin and a small animal waist – mink.

There was a lot of back pain and I knew the bones were in the wrong place, that they sometimes nudged up against other bones, trapped nerves and caused the rest of my body to sit out of alignment. That is what Andrea said.

She and I grew up together in the woods at the end of our street, woods of larch, pine and spruce, and that one white incisor, that single, exquisite silver birch. We built dens together out of the rubbish that was dumped in the woods, along with sticks and logs, pine needles and big daubs of mud in the winter. We made everything together.

If it is possible to imagine integrity – the kind that most human beings are deficient in – then it is possible to imagine Andrea. She often said to me that her generosity was a cover, that she gave of herself in order that people thought well of her. But I watched how she tended to her ailing mother without grumbling and expected nothing in return. Her mother might spill her food a dozen times and Andrea would clean it up a dozen times. As her condition worsened, it was the loss of independence that her mother struggled with most of all. Andrea saw this and respected it.

Who am I compared to Andrea?

4

In the wake of Andrea's disappearance, Mark McAdam became the focal point of one of the hysterical stories concocted by the local community. I knew that McAdam, whoever he was, had done nothing wrong, and I watched as he tried to extricate himself from the web of lies that was being woven around him.

People like to know the truth. People like certainty and clarity – especially when they are afraid – and so, during the first weeks of the investigation, McAdam served a useful purpose. He was a stranger to the area. Nobody knew anything about him, so it was easy to attach blame, to indict and demonise. Where there is no understanding, there is harsh judgement. I know this truth very well, not least because I grew up believing what my parents impressed upon me: that I was lacking in something, something I would never be able to retrieve. I would never move across the waters of my life *completely*.

The story of McAdam always makes me smile. It was ironic in many ways: people sought certainty in the least certain place.

Andrea had told me about McAdam in the late summer – our last summer in the woods before her disappearance – when the trees were just beginning to turn. She had laughed so hard about their encounter. I do not know why, because it seemed eerie to me and inexplicable, things which most people find discomforting. But Andrea was not like most people.

McAdam had turned up at Andrea's door one day, seemingly out of the blue. She said he had introduced himself as though he was an old friend, and when Andrea showed no sign of recognising him, he persevered, 'It's me, Mark. Mark McAdam. We met on the retreat last year. Don't you remember? Heidi introduced me to you…'

But Andrea had no memory of McAdam. None at all. If she had been a woman who was easily frightened or suspicious by nature, she would have shut the door in his face. But he was persistent, and she was fascinated by the uncanny nature of his story.

'We walked up the mountain together, the three of us,' he said. 'You must remember that? The big mountain at the back of the retreat centre. It was a hot day and you forgot to bring your water bottle… Heidi got a stitch halfway up. I remember because you were wearing a pink hat with a swan on it. Or a goose, I can't remember exactly…'

Andrea did have a pink hat with a swan on it, and she did have a friend called Heidi who also attended the caregivers' retreats; and the centre did have a mountain at its back; and she had climbed it with Heidi. She remembered all of that, she said, but she had no memory of McAdam. She told me she had looked closely at his face. She had made eye contact with him and held his gaze, but there was no flicker of recognition. Her body did not respond. Her mind could not recall anything.

McAdam had continued to recollect specific details of their time on retreat together, but the more he spoke, the more amused Andrea became. She assumed that he must have met Heidi and learnt all this information from her. How else could he know so much about her?

She was laughing so hard when she told me, that it was several minutes before she was able to catch her breath and speak normally.

'What did he want from you, then?' I asked.

'I don't know. Maybe he was lonely.'

'Or scheming.'

'Maybe he was trying to sell me something? Why else do strange men turn up at your door?'

'He might have been dangerous.'

'He didn't seem the type.'

According to Andrea, he had looked at her with a mixture of concern and frustration.

'He thought I'd gone mad. He really believed I'd lost my mind.' But Andrea never missed a trick. She was the most astute person I knew. 'He got upset in the end. I thought he was going to cry right there on my doorstep, in his old jeans and stained T-shirt.'

'He sounds like a tramp.'

'He was clean-shaven, good teeth, not your standard kind of tramp.' She turned to me and grinned with her teeth showing in a silly, exaggerated smile. 'Sometimes I wonder what would've happened if I'd welcomed him in as an old friend.'

I picked up a pine cone and turned it around in my palm.

'What do you mean, Andrea? I wish you were serious about it, instead of always making it into a joke.'

'It was just some freak incident, don't you see? Some random bloke, that's all.'

When McAdam became implicated in Andrea's disappearance, the retreat centre was contacted and his name was found on the list of participants for the previous year, just as he had said. Heidi was also contacted and corroborated McAdam's story.

What had really happened?

How is it that the mind forgets some things and retains others?

5

It rained for five years and when it finally stopped, I had become more mud than man. Martin was standing over me in a dark blue, almost black uniform and it was broad daylight. When I looked up at the birch tree, I noticed the huge moth had gone.

'It's addressed to you, Quinn,' Martin said, handing me the paper envelope.

His name tag read 'M. Payne' in black lettering. He smiled as though there was something benevolent behind the uniform.

'You've to go to the Medical Centre.'

'But there is nothing wrong with me.'

'All the same.'

Martin was taller than me. He had a brown moustache the colour of milky coffee and he smelt of cheap aftershave or shower gel – Imperial Leather. He stood like a man in uniform stands: pelvis, chest, chin.

'Hurry up! We haven't got all day.'

When I stood up, I realised my strange coat was covered in mud. My trousers and boots were covered in mud. I realised I did not like Martin and I did not want to have anything to do with him. He was threatening. There was something about his manner that made me uncomfortable. It was as though everything that was happening was happening *to* me, that I had no say in the matter. I did not like the way his face was shiny. I did not like his small round eyes, black and glistening. I hated mice.

'I'll escort you over and bring you back,' he said.

I was worried about Andrea, but Martin was waiting, tapping the face of his watch. He had a radio strapped to his belt and a black pouch of keys.

'You hungry?'

I stuffed the paper envelope in my pocket and followed him back the way we had come.

6

The corridor was strip-lit and empty. I walked alongside Martin, feeling nothing. Sometimes the smell of the corridor got to me – stale sweat masked by acrid cleaning products – but I was beyond caring. My muddy boots left marks on the lino. There was nobody about.

We turned left at the end of the corridor and headed to a part of the basement that was unfamiliar to me.

'That's where they're seeing you,' he said, nodding towards an old door with a small metal grille, 'down there.'

He unlocked the door and put his head on one side like an inquisitive bird. I was to go in.

The crows came for me at once. At least, I think they were crows. They might have been ravens or rooks – I was too busy defending myself to notice. Whichever of the corvids is the most vicious, it was that one.

An overhead light was on and there was a big wooden desk
in the middle of the room, two chairs and a glass lamp with
no shade, switched off but clearly meant to illuminate the
pile of papers lying there. The birds had spoilt everything.

I did not think they could do me much harm to begin with,
but there were three of them and they were big, seagull size,
with strong beaks and small black eyes. They flapped around
the room at ankle height and then bounced up to peck me,
repeatedly going for the pale flesh of my face, as though they
did not like the colour of it. Then they flew at the base of the
lamp and stabbed it, over and over, until their beaks bled and
small red spurts of it flicked over the desk, the papers and floor.

Without arms, I would have suffered more. They bounced
and flew in relay, passing my face like a baton from one bird
to the next as they circled, attacking the lamp and then me
by turns. Without arms, I would have lost an eye for sure,
maybe both.

I called repeatedly to Martin but he did not respond. I did not
know whether he was waiting on the other side of the door
or not. In any case, nobody came when I banged to be let out.

The sound of a woman praying

7

I had done nothing wrong.

A woman entered and proceeded to collect up the crows. They were docile with her, like pets, and hopped towards her as she made a sucking noise with her mouth, the kind of sound women use to call a cat. She put them in a cardboard box and closed the lid. I could hear them flapping and scratching their vicious beaks and claws against the sides of the box. I watched as she efficiently cleared the desk, opened a drawer and pulled out some papers. She had a brooch in the shape of a bird pinned to her lapel. I was hunched in one corner in my strange coat and muddy boots, tending my wounds.

'How are you feeling, Quinn?'

'Who are you?'

'Anna.'

I snorted because that was my mother's name.

My arms and hands were scratched and bruised, and when I felt my face I could tell the skin was broken just beneath my right eye.

Anna said nothing for a minute or two, and I watched her breathe, her chest rising and falling. She was otherwise so motionless and expressionless that her breathing was the only way I knew she was alive; everything else about her seemed dead, unreal. I could not speak to a dead person. I could not unburden myself, or whatever it was she wanted me to do. You need real people for that.

Anna had a small, nasty face – dark blue, almost black eyes, whiskers on her top lip and a few on her chin. She reminded me of a schoolteacher. She had her legs crossed at the ankles, brown tights, neat black shoes with no heel.

'I have no time for this. I need to find Andrea.'

'Andrea's dead, Quinn. You know that.'

I was looking for the smile at the corner of her mouth, but it was not there. Her cheeks flushed a little. I tried to look her in the eye but she averted her gaze, shuffled papers. Her breasts were big.

'Your appeal has been turned down.'

'What are you talking about?'

'Your appeal, Quinn, for a retrial.'

She passed me a letter with my name at the top and I glanced down at the signature – some solicitor named Braithwaite.

'All you have to do is sign here.'

She handed me a second piece of paper.

'It's just to say that we've met, that I've given you the letter, told you what's what.'

My hands were hanging like dead fish. I could tell that I looked sallow, pathetic.

8

Five years passed, or the sun and the moon had tricked me. I must have been imagining things, although being in this place was enough to make anyone mad.

Sometimes the mind tricks us into believing things that are not real. For some reason, it made me think of Adolf Eichmann and all the other men at the Wannsee Conference, those high-ranking Nazi and German government officials who agreed upon the Final Solution. From a psychiatric perspective, they were not mentally ill or unstable – their behaviour was inexplicable. No matter how much psychology tried to straighten it out or to find an answer for the people left behind to hold on to, it was no good. Some things are not deducible.

What happened with Anna fell into this category. With no prompting from me, she lay down on the desk and invited me to touch her. I did not feel OK about it. She was an ugly woman, even if her breasts were big.

The desk was not long enough for her whole body, so her legs were hanging off one end, bent at the knee. I could see her brown tights more clearly. Her shoes were twinkling – dark, patent leather.

No doubt it was because I did not know what to do that I started to laugh. It was a deep chuckle to begin with and then it got louder and louder as I tried to resist it. I suppose it is true to say that I was in shock. I laughed very hard until my belly hurt and I had to put the Braithwaite letter down and rest my hands on my back. I was swaying about like a puppet.

When the fit had passed, I looked closely at Anna. She did not appear to have moved. The desk was making a grating sound, groaning under the weight of her, even though – apart from her breasts – she was not a big woman. It was as though the desk had a life of its own, had suffered enough. She lay quite still, the front of her jacket slipping open. I wiped the tears from my eyes and reached out a hand to her face. She did not respond. The overhead light was so bright it made her skin look fluorescent. She looked like a plastic doll. I did not want to look at her eyes. Some part of me knew that there was that flatness around the eyes that I do not like, the way aluminium goes when it oxidises – no sheen. It was as though she had dirty teaspoons for eyes.

I had done nothing wrong.

9

It was Martin who brought me back to my dank little cell. He did not speak to me and would not look me in the eye. Perhaps he felt guilty because my face was bleeding. There was one particularly painful peck mark just beneath my right eye. It was deep and I could put the tip of my little finger inside it and feel the wetness. A throbbing, stinging pain, and that vulnerable, gashed feeling that comes when a wound is open to the air.

He did not mention Anna and nor did I.

I had sat down at my little desk in the corner, more from weariness than anything else, and I heard Martin pull the door shut behind him and lock it.

There was a thin, insipid line of sunlight on the concrete floor, shining in through the slit. I watched it for a few minutes.

When the sun comes in like that, it always reminds me of Balram Farah's dog, the day in his house when we drank endless cups of tea and the dog sprawled on the carpet, its body positioned to absorb the maximum sunlight beaming in through the double-glazed windows. There is still much to tell of Farah and his dog.

The weariness was always there, a dark boulder in my brain. I laid the letter out on the desk. Braithwaite. It reminded me that Martin had given me the moth, and I pulled the crumpled paper envelope from my pocket and stared at it. It was muddy and damp and smelt of lavender. I did not recognise the handwriting on the envelope. I dropped it onto the desk with the other.

10

Let it be known that I have suffered.

The weariness and the hunger dragged me down. As time passed, I had no memory of a good meal. I could not remember the taste of real food, a mouthful of chicken, a well-cooked potato, greens fresh from a garden. None of this was available to me and I resented it.

When I was seven years old, my father gave me a birthday present. He had never done this before and he never did it again. Perhaps it was because my mother had dared a small disagreement, even reprobation. I do not know. It was a remarkable moment in my childhood, not only because it was a singular gesture of love, but because it was the first and only time I took an animal's life for food.

It *was* love. It was the only way my father knew how to love, and a part of me knew that this limitation of his did not make him a bad man. Somehow, he loved me; at least this is the story I tell myself now.

The birthday present was a live chicken in a cardboard box, a small brown hen with a red comb, and I remember her well. After I had opened the box in the kitchen, my father gave me two options: either I was to wring the bird's neck or I was to axe the head from the body. Either way, I was then to pluck and eviscerate the bird and make it ready for the dinner table.

My mother had gone to church. Apart from the brown hen, the kitchen was lifeless, and my brother was upstairs in his sickbed, where he always was. It was a moment in which my father and I were all but dead; neither one of us was truly there, or so it seemed to me.

I do not want to say that the killing was easy. I do not want to say that the killing was hard. It was neither of these things. It was frightening. The bird knew that its life was about to end, even though I was only seven years old and barely able to lift an axe, let alone hold the bird still while I hacked at its rangy neck. There was blood, enough to remind me that life was too much for Quinn, that he was bound to fail.

My father taught me to heat a pot of water to sixty-five degrees Celsius – too hot and the skin of the chicken will tear during plucking; too cool and the feathers will not come away – and to dip the dead chicken into the hot water for a minute or two, just until the leg feathers let go, the cue that the bird is ready to be plucked.

I have not forgotten these details. I remember the eyes of the bird as though it were only yesterday that I killed it. I remember the softness of the feathers and its helplessness in the hands of a creature so much bigger and stronger than it. It fought for its life as if life were a diamond jewel, something shining, something full of promise and worth; as if nothing else in the world was more valuable. A part of me envied the chicken this passionate struggle.

When my mother came home, she tutted and scolded me. There was a little blood on the kitchen floor, a stray feather here and there, even though I had done the killing outside.

The table was laid for dinner and the chicken was roasted. I was not hungry but my father put one of the chicken's wings on my plate. He said it was an honour to eat the wing of a bird I had killed and prepared, but it did not feel honourable to me. As soon as I was allowed to leave the table, I threw the wing up and went to see my brother.

My father did not mention the gift again. Sometimes, I imagine that he was proud of me for killing the bird.

If that wing were on my plate now, I would not hesitate to eat it. I would give anything to eat fresh roasted meat. I am not by nature a trader, but there are some things a man cannot live without.

11

I was locked in. There is nothing clean about being locked in. There is nothing just about being locked in. Nobody in his right mind would lock someone in a concrete cell barely big enough for a dog. How does it feel, I wonder, to walk away from a cell that you have locked, inside of which is a man? How does it feel to go to sleep at night, knowing that you have locked a man away? It must be a strange power and an unsettling reminder: this man could be any man, could, in fact, be you. If the person who locks a man away has a heart that beats, then they must be frightened by the fear their keys create. It is not easy being a prisoner and it is not easy being the one who imprisons. Perhaps it is because there is little difference between them? Perhaps in fact they are just the same?

Whatever they were saying about me was a lie. It was likely that all sorts of stories had been made up to castigate me. As with Mark McAdam, people invented things when they did not know the truth or when they were desperate to cling on to something, even if it was outlandish. People do not like uncertainty, or to be made to feel out of control.

Perhaps Andrea's mother had maligned me – it was her testament that had indicted me, after all. It was infuriating, not least because I could not clear my name from inside this concrete cell. Sometimes, there was this fire in me, an inferno of rage that felt as though it had no beginning and no end. Sometimes I could feel the seething in my gut, and as the breath passed in and out of my body, the bitter-tasting gall rose to my mouth. It was not the kind of fire that Andrea had.

I staggered to the door and hammered on it with what little strength I had left. There was no response, not even the sound of a distant door opening and closing.

12

It was God's own truth that when I woke in the morning, the sun was rising in the west. Either that or I was imagining things. Being in this place was enough to make anyone mad.

Sitting up was painful, as though my limbs had been torn from my body and clumsily reattached. I put my feet flat on the cold concrete floor and stared out through the slit. If there had been a mirror, I would have inspected the rainbow of bruises and stab marks. My eyes had bled a little; the peck wounds had oozed in the night.

I was hungrier and wearier than I had ever been. My strange coat had dried and the mud had flaked off over the bed and floor. Somebody had taken the laces out of my boots, which stood by the door.

I tried to urinate in the tin bucket, but the thimbleful of fluid seemed to travel backwards up my urethra. Even though the bucket was empty, it stank and there was no means of rinsing it out. There was no water, no sink, no soap. I could neither drown myself nor quench my thirst. My body was shrivelling like a desert flower.

It was possible that I imagined the door opening and the man coming in. I did not remember hearing a key make contact with the lock. I did not remember the turning sound nor the habitual creak of the hinges as the bulk of metal swung wide.

It was not Martin. The man was not wearing a uniform, but what looked like two bulky grey dressing gowns, one on top of the other. He had thin hair that was stuck to his head with sweat or blood – it was hard to tell which. He looked at me slowly with a kind of behind-eyes-looking that only some people possess. Like a seer.

He closed the door behind him, hobbled into the cell without speaking and beckoned me over to the far corner, furthest away from the slit. It was as if he was intimately familiar with the space and knew there was something here worth investigating. It was only three steps but it felt further, like I was going somewhere I had never been before, with a breeze coming in through the slit and the cell floor leading outside. But when I stood still, I realised it was not true. In fact, I was standing in the grimy half-light with a man I did not know, someone who seemed more insect than human.

'Take your time,' he said.

He was not being sarcastic. He said it as though he knew the three steps were very far indeed, as though whatever I had previously thought about the distance between the bed and the desk or the desk and the slit, was wrong.

Nobody had ever said, 'Take your time,' to me before, at least not like that. I was thrown by how he said the words. I suppose you could say they were kind, but I am not sure. After everything that has happened, I do not know if kindness is what it was.

The man was standing in the corner with his back to the wall, shoulders relaxed, as if he had been standing there for decades. His eyelids were drooping. He looked like he needed a nap, but not the kind of naps I took, not the heavy nap that comes from the deep, dark space of the gut and the bowel. Evidently, he was going to snooze in the corner until I had taken the time he seemed to think I needed.

The man did not move or say anything else. He did not try to persuade or entice me. He just stood there dozing, his eyes flickering open occasionally, like a flea with half an eye on its host. I did not ask him anything – I wish I had now – I just looked. I noticed the thinness of his nose and the way his hands hung like dead fish. Everything about him was thin. The bulk of two dressing gowns did nothing to make his form strong and solid. I could have picked him up with one hand and posted him through the slit. His limbs were built of sparrow bones. His chest was a pigeon's.

I stood and stared at him for a long time. There was something familiar about him, but I did not feel afraid. Slowly, imperceptibly at first, the man began to dissolve into the wall. There was no cracking or crumbling or smashing – the wall simply hollowed out to make space for him, forming an alcove like the ones in churches where the Madonna and Christ child stand. The strange man stepped back into the recess and stood like a statue. I watched as his body turned slowly to stone, the same grey as the concrete walls. The skin of his face stretched and smoothed out. I moved closer to get a better look.

When I touched his face, it was definitely stone, and his body, draped as it was in his two stone dressing gowns, was hunched in the alcove as though it had been there forever. I tapped his cheek, waited to see if anything would happen if I touched his mouth. Nothing.

I could hear the blood in my head. It had started to rain and I could smell it through the slit.

Stone Man was waiting for something. What did he know about waiting?

13

Five years passed, or the sun and the moon had tricked me, and I woke to find a small cloth bag on my pillow. I picked it up and turned it over. It was pale pink and smelt strongly of lavender. I squished it between my finger and thumb – it was lavender all right; I could feel the separate buds.

There were several minutes in which I felt more at home in my body than I had for years. I remembered my hands and face, my nose, as though they were astonishing, extraordinary. There have been times in my life when the body has shown itself to me as a miracle. It was Andrea who made me aware of the intricacy of the human form; of the power that it held, not just because it was a biological phenomenon of profound complexity, but because it was a gift that enabled me to exist alongside her.

I stared at the small bag and inhaled its scent.

I could hear Martin approaching – his one stiff hip – so I threw the bag onto the floor. Flowers would be confiscated. Anything organic would be removed, except the invisible creatures I existed alongside, and the microscopic organisms that lived on me. They could not be taken away.

'What's the matter with you, Quinn?' He looked quizzically at the stabs and bruises on my face. 'Will I have to take you to the Medical Centre?'

His face was deadpan; there was no irony or threat in his voice. He looked kind, as though he genuinely wanted to help me.

'No, Martin.'

'It's your choice.'

Except it was not.

He looked the cell up and down, the same as every day, making sure, double-checking: grey concrete walls, bed, desk, chair, bucket, slit; and Stone Man. Stone Man was still hunched in his recess, but Martin never said anything about him. Perhaps he had been there all along and I had been too intent on finding Andrea to notice.

'What's that?'

'A lavender bag.'

'Very funny.'

He watched me from the doorway as I turned my head to look at it. The door was open and I could see all the way down the corridor. I could see the sheen of the lino in the gloom, and the dark red line that ran the length of the walls at hip height.

'It has nothing to do with me.'

'Pick it up and give it here!'

'You get it!'

I was sitting on the edge of the bed, but I got up slowly and went to sit at the desk, as far away from the lavender bag as I could get. The chair squeaked as I sat down.

'Get the fuck up and bring me that thing! Now!'

'No.'

I liked Martin. He was never excessively abusive.

He did not know what to do. He stood in the doorway, thinking and bristling. If he had been an animal, he would have been a porcupine. For a few seconds, the cell became my room again and I felt my body relax. It was morning, my favourite time of the day, and spring was here, the most hopeful season.

'Quinn, I'm not going to ask you again…'

Poor Martin. He probably did not know how to go down on a woman. He probably ate Rice Krispies for his breakfast. I could tell that his uniform was too tight, that his hip was hurting. And I was glad.

'What's the matter with you, Quinn? It's not a big deal. Just pick the thing up and bring it here. Then it's over.'

He shifted his weight from right to left.

'You know it's against policy for me to come in and get it without another officer being present. Come on, be a good man and do what I'm asking.'

Martin was good at changing tack. He was not as stupid as I first thought he was. He seemed to know that ratcheting up the anger brought out the brute in me, and then there was nowhere left to go.

I got up nonchalantly and picked up the bag. It felt damp and no longer smelt of lavender. I passed it to Martin, glad I no longer had to deal with it. But as I handed it to him and he bent his head to study it, something crossed over in me and I bolted. The door was open. Martin should have been more cautious.

I had no idea where I was going or how to get out. The only walkway I knew was the corridor to the basement. Everything else was unknown. But I knew how to run. Even though I'd been shut up for so long, I still knew how to run.

Martin raised the alarm immediately. He was good at his job.

I had about forty-five seconds, perhaps sixty seconds of running, but it felt longer than all the time I had been kept apart from Andrea. I was the proverbial arrow leaving the bow. Who was the archer?

My bony body jumped the last flight of steps and I landed in the basement. I had time to try two of the dark blue doors before they kicked me to the ground and twisted my arms back for the cuffs. They had red faces and smelt of sweat.

The last time I ran flat out like that was when my brother died. The sun was out and I remember thinking how warm it was, how good to have sunlight after the long winter. Then the call came and the first thing I wanted to do was run. I did not want to speak to anyone nor see anyone nor hold anyone. I wanted to run flat out to the hospital, about half a mile away, to see my brother's face one last time before they put him in the ground.

He looked like I thought he would look: mousy, skeletal. His hair was lank, stuck to his head with sweat or blood – it was hard to tell which. The room smelt of bleach and someone had shut the dark blue curtains. The walls and the trolley bed were waiting for us to breathe. When I looked at my brother, he no longer seemed real.

Five years passed, or the sun and the moon had tricked me, and I stayed by his bed, sweating profusely. Drops of sweat fell onto the white sheet, moistened the skin of his small white hand. It was not an unexpected death, but that did not make it easier to bear. Each time my brother had smiled at me, some distant part of me had returned. He was like my sibling horse, one who could comfort and call me back; one who understood the need to escape, galloping at full tilt. He had been ill all his life and I had been the healthy son, the one who should have known better. The one who needed to learn to give up his life for another, to put himself aside without extinguishing himself altogether.

A nurse came in and remarked on the heat. She opened a window and then handed me a towel from the end of the bed. She offered no condolences. I liked that.

I was grateful to the lavender bag for those sixty seconds of running.

14

It is true that liars cannot heal. I had known this truth for many years, many generations. It was a truth handed down. This truth does not tire of being truthful and it asks of every man that he lie down on the earth with his deeds. This truth is a dark blue truth, almost black.

I had woken from a bad dream in which the lavender bag was pressed up against my face and out of it hundreds of white maggots were squirming. It felt as though my cheeks were rotting and the maggots were feeding off me. I could feel their slow, munching progress on my flesh. I brushed them off – *plip, plip, plip* on the concrete floor – but every time I brushed, another hundred appeared in their place.

Do not misjudge me.

15

At an ungodly hour, the light went on. It was brighter than usual and not just because it woke me from sleep. The cell was stifling. A bare bulb hung from the ceiling like a tiny exploding sun. I blinked into the light expecting to see Martin, but there was nobody there.

I got out of bed, peeled the sweaty clothes from my body and went over to the slit. I stood on tiptoes and strained to peer out.

Then a flash, followed shortly after by another. Stone Man was moving around the cell, climbing on the bed, the desk, crouching back in the alcove, squatting on the floor; and from every position he took a photograph of me. He held what looked like an old-fashioned SLR and took picture after picture, sometimes with a flash, sometimes without.

It did not have to bother me. These kinds of irrelevant activities never usually bothered me. And I was doing nothing but standing beneath the slit. No photograph could indict me.

Stone Man was taking pictures of me from every angle. The lens was zooming in on my nose and eyes, my collarbone, my genitals, in fact on every part of my gaunt, white body.

He was silent at his work and when I said to him to stop, he continued in silence, taking even more pictures even more quickly, as though every inch of my skin and hair had to be photographed, had to be captured for someone else to look at. It felt like the body I had was a joke body, the kind of thing people would hang on a wall and throw darts at.

Every time I moved to grab the camera from his hands, he seemed to evaporate and reappear in a different part of the cell. He was slippery, unassailable. I was breathing heavily, speeding up my movements to try to catch him unawares, but each time I moved he took another photograph and rewound the shutter release. I could hear the whirr and click of the instrument, louder and louder.

If this was my body, I no longer wanted it. If this was my slack belly, my flaccid penis, my loose, unhelpful limbs, I no longer wanted to call them mine. I no longer wanted to own this shrunken, hanging backside, these pin legs, these fingers made of useless wire. Most of all, I did not want Stone Man to see me, to see these imperfections in the stark light, and to photograph them over and over as if to record how grotesque I was, how ugly and pointless and lame.

The lens bore into me. I felt my skin begin to burn as the penetration of the viewer deepened.

This was my cell, my bed, my desk, but Stone Man was oblivious, showed no respect for privacy. He had dark blue eyes that quivered and jerked from one shot to the next. It was as though he had been a photojournalist all his life, as though nothing could have been more natural.

I was breathing so rapidly, my heart was in my ears and in my throat. Its colour seeped into the cell, turning the light red, turning Stone Man red, even the concrete walls, and then my mind flooded with Andrea and the woods. The silver birch where we met on Fridays, year after year, grew tall and red.

This was not what I had chosen for my life. I did not come here because I wanted to or because there was nothing better to do. I came here because there was no choice. I was a wheel from which every spoke had been torn out.

16

It was God's own truth that when I woke in the morning, the sun was rising in the west. Either that or I was imagining things. Being in this place was enough to make anyone mad.

The cell was the same as before, but the walls were different. Stone Man had returned to his perch in the alcove, but the walls were plastered with photographs. Every inch of wall was covered. Everywhere I looked I saw myself, or a part of me. Limb, torso, sex. I was mortified.

I turned my back to Stone Man and lay with my strange coat pulled over my head.

Let it be known that I have suffered. I was familiar with suffering in the way only some men are – it was in my blood.

Beneath the cave of my coat, I could smell the foulness of my breath. I could feel the heavy stench moving in and out of my lungs, and it repulsed me. I resolved to focus exclusively on the slit, to blur out the walls and whatever might be hanging there. But it did not last long. The photographs were there and I could not stop myself from looking.

I was black and white with no borders. The images went all the way to the edge. I stared, fascinated by the shape of the legs, my thighs, the place where my penis rested in a small shadow, slightly blurred. I walked the four walls of the cell looking closely at each picture. My hair was longer than I had thought. I was growing a very big beard. Some of the pictures were a regular size but others were blown up. A shot of my right eye had been so enlarged, it looked like a fish in a gloomy river or some deep, distant sea. It was out of focus, discomforting.

But as is the way with the human mind, it was no time before I discovered something smooth and unthreatening about the photographs, and I felt a small sense of relief return to me: nobody but Stone Man would see the images, and besides, they were not dangerous.

Indeed, the more I looked, the more I wanted to look, and soon I was glad that Stone Man had taken these pictures and stuck them to the wall of my cell. There was nothing else to do – why should I not delight in my own image, in the intricacies of flesh and hair and bone?

I shifted quietly from one wall to the next, perusing my gallery, gradually and then swiftly becoming more and more aroused.

Afterwards, the pain in my penis was excruciating. Likewise, my hands and arms ached with pain, a kind of deep, heavy pummelling inside my veins. It was like the blood there was trying to clot. Even thinking was painful.

17

Ejaculation always reminded me of Libby. I do not remember her surname. No, it reminded me of the tramp who assaulted her many years ago.

It happened in our local town, in the big park with the lake surrounded by tall birch and pine. It was a four-mile walk from our street, and I used to go there in the summer after school to be on my own and think about things for myself. It was often quiet in the park, even on warm summer nights. People preferred to sit inside their houses, something I have never understood. The four walls of a building can oppress a man.

I was fourteen and still wearing the old shorts my mother had made for me two years earlier. They were too tight and too short that year, and by the time I had walked from the street to the park, they had chafed a thin red line around my thighs. I stood by the lake, wishing I could take them off and walk in my underpants, but I did not dare to expose myself.

The lake was home to ducks – mostly mallards – and in the winter, the whooper swans. My mother used to complain about the swans because they made a mess of the grass banks, but I liked them, not least because they left feathers behind. I would take them home and wash them carefully, running the vanes under the tap to watch how the water ran off the surface. Feathers are so clever like that, so immune to downpour or immersion.

One winter I found a wing feather as long as my forearm, the quill almost as thick as my baby finger. It was a prize possession for many years until, in a drunken stupor, my father tried to write with it, cutting the quill to form a nib and dipping it into dark blue gloss paint. I suppose he thought he was being funny. The feather never recovered and nor did my father – he was rarely sober after that.

There was a young woman – a girl I later recognised as Libby from school – sunbathing beside the lake. She was wearing a red bikini and her skin was very white. Her bicycle was leaning up against a nearby tree and she was lying still with a book and black sunglasses that covered most of the upper half of her face. She would burn if she was not careful. Even in the evening, the sun was hot and fierce. A person could get sunstroke or severe burns from the penetration of the sun's rays. A part of me wanted to warn her, but then I realised this is what my mother would have done. I walked over to a cedar of Lebanon and sat down in its generous shade.

Was she dozing? Did she not hear the man approach?

I had seen him before in the park. He was what my mother would have called a tramp, with clothes that were held together by the stench of urine, alcohol and sweat. Most of his face was a beard. I saw that he had opened his trousers – such as they were – and he was kneeling over the young woman, pumping himself quickly against her body. His backside was a white shock.

It did not last very long because the girl kicked and pushed so much that he fell to the side, his trousers around his ankles. She was making a sound halfway between sobbing and screaming. I remember her body was shaking and I watched as she scrambled to get on her bike and ride away.

She left behind the towel that she was lying on and the book, which had a dark blue cover, almost black. I never could remember the title and I ponder it now and again. Who picked the book up? Who read the words that had witnessed so much fear and harm?

I cannot recall this time without shame. Sometimes I wonder if I have remembered correctly. It is such a long time ago and memory is unreliable, of course.

I told Andrea what I had seen and she immediately knew who the girl was. For days after the incident, she tried to persuade Libby to report the tramp to the police, but she was too afraid and did not want her parents to find out. In the end, Andrea and Libby went to the police station together and reported what had happened. The officers nodded and scribbled a few words down – names, date.

I had done nothing wrong.

18

The weariness and the hunger slumped over me like a needy ghost. It was unapologetic. It had eyes that violated my dreams, my thoughts, my bones. Sometimes this brought me consolation, since I thought Stone Man must feel it too. Stone Man could not be immune to everything. I imagined the hunger scraping channels in the stone of his brain. It felt good. It gave me hope that one day he would also be too weary to keep going and would finally leave.

It was not me who was taking his time.

19

Five years passed, or the sun and the moon had tricked me. A moth had flown in through the slit and landed on the bed beside me. I hated moths, but I did not swipe it away. I had to admit that it was a beautiful thing, with four iridescent, blue-ringed eyes and amber patches on its wings. Emperor moth. It seemed impossible that something this small and fragile could be so beautiful. Its wings were as thin as paper and its tiny body could have been crushed with one thumb.

Do not lay up for yourselves treasures on earth, where moth and rust destroy and where thieves break in and steal; but lay up for yourselves treasures in heaven, where neither moth nor rust destroys and where thieves do not break in and steal. For where your treasure is, there your heart will be also.

The Gospel of Matthew. My mother always recited this passage whenever she saw a moth. She would mutter the words under her breath so that my father did not hear. But I heard.

It is still pathetic to me now that I took so long to remember the moth that Martin had given me all that time ago. I must have been absent for so much of my incarceration. I wasted many years in this manner.

The paper envelope had sat unopened on my desk through rain and shine. Light had fallen on it, darkness had fallen on it, and I had passed it by every day without curiosity, without faith, without lifeblood. There it lay, a plank of driftwood on an insignificant ocean, until the emperor moth arrived.

I picked the paper envelope up and placed it immediately under my nose. There was no remaining scent of lavender. I wiped a thin layer of dust from its surface. My name was printed on it in block capitals, in a hand that I did not recognise. I turned it over and unpeeled the lip.

Inside was not one letter, but a long series of letters from Andrea's mother. The letters were written – some of them were scrawled – on old-fashioned airmail paper, pale blue and so thin they were like the wings of the moth. As I opened the sheets one by one, they seemed to grow in number. They spilled from the envelope as though they were living voices, shouting and beseeching, softening and raging. At times, I had to put the sheets down on the table and walk over to the slit, in order to be able to breathe.

I did not like the experience of hearing her words. I did not like the way in which my body responded. Inside my gut, something was not right. There was so much pain coming from the sheets of paper and this pain seemed to travel inside me. If I had to speak of my heart, I would say that it was imploding inside my chest. It was like a bird's egg held in the clenched fist of an angry, unforgiving human. I could not get away from this feeling of implosion. I tried very hard to get away, but I did not manage it.

There were lines and expressions that have stayed with me. One of the early letters – they were written over a period of six years – was so violent in its outburst, so damning in its righteous judgement of me, that I had to sit down and stand up, sit down and stand up many times over, to take my mind off the agony of her mistake: I was not the man she thought I was. She had stuck me inside a completely rigid container, one that only she was able to define and justify, and she was so entirely convinced that she was right, that any and all behaviour or expression on her part became vindicated. 'You are a vile, worthless individual,' she wrote, never allowing me to be equal.

It is true that a part of me did also begin to believe her. It took me many days to read all the letters, and many more to reread them. It was difficult to be so loathed and to have that loathing whisper out from the sheets into the cell, all day and all night. It was difficult to be so misjudged. It felt as though I had two choices and they were both unhelpful: either I railed in anger against her righteousness or I began to believe she was right. It did not occur to me that there might be other options, and it was some long time before I was able to accommodate anything else.

In one of the later letters, she wrote of being so broken, 'like an open wound that is repeatedly bludgeoned', that she could barely bring herself to communicate anymore. Indeed, it was the briefest letter in the series. A few scribbled lines in blue ink, most of the words blurred and smudged, so that it took some deciphering to work out what she had written. There were many times that I wished I had not bothered.

And then there was the final letter. I had not expected it. No, there was not one iota of me that suspected what was to come. Even during the days of rereading the letters, the content of the final one did not really hit home. I was unable to comprehend what was being said, and the enormity of the implications of her letter was, to begin with, quite beyond me.

Quinn,

This is the last letter I'm writing to you. These past six years have been a long and horrific journey. I've never hated a human being as much as I've hated you. You took away the one person in my life I loved beyond all others. I miss her every day, think about her every day. I've cried so much my head still hasn't stopped aching. I thought I was going to die of heartache and I wanted to die.

You'll have read of the many days that I've cursed you. I can't pretend that there aren't still times I wish you dead. But as the years have passed and grief has emptied me, I've come to realise – slowly and with a fierce reluctance – that there's only one means to truly heal the pain and loss that you've brought to my life: somehow I have to find a way to forgive you. God help me!

Andrea was my only child, as you know. These letters don't even begin to tell you how my life has been devastated by her absence. I hold you fully responsible for the end of my daughter's life, and I want you to know what that means. I want you, on some level, to understand the consequences of your actions.

You know of course that Andrea was not only my daughter but also my carer. Since you took her away from me, I've been tended day and night by professional carers. They've done an excellent job. They've fed and dressed me. They've pushed me out in the sun and talked to me when life became unbearable. I'm grateful to these carers for their kindness and their commitment to work that's not always rewarding. It's hard work, relentless and often tragic. But for all their care and genuine concern for my well-being, they're not my daughter. They don't speak with her words. They don't laugh with her laughter. They don't cry with her tears.

I don't know how to forgive you, but I'm finally prepared to try. I'm not sure what that means, except that this forgiveness is for me, not you. There's something in it that seems to relieve me, a kind of letting go, I suppose – not of the pain, but of the constant replay of the pain. Without some kind of forgiveness, you're a cancer festering inside me and I refuse to be held to ransom like this for the rest of my life. Bitterness and anger make for a sordid, barbaric life, as you must surely understand. I refuse to turn into the kind of person that Andrea would not have liked. It would feel too much like betrayal.

In recent months, I've spent time – like you, I've ample time to consider things – thinking about forgiveness: saying 'I forgive you' is one thing, making it real, quite another. What can I do to relieve even some of this pain? After long and agonising consideration – I can barely believe I'm writing this – I realised that one way through would be to invite you into my home as my carer, to stand in Andrea's stead. It's a ridiculous idea, of course, but for some reason that makes it all the more appropriate.

I've been reading about a woman whose young son was shot dead by a rival gang member. It was what the gangs call 'a rite of passage killing' – brutal and abhorrent on every level. The killer was incarcerated for some years – I can't remember how many – and over time the mother of the dead son began to visit him in prison. First of all, she wanted to see who had taken her son's life. She wanted to see not just the person who'd stood in the dock, but the real person, the small person beneath the front, the vulnerable person beneath the skin and bone and flesh. She visited him for years, taking small gifts – things he'd requested and things he hadn't. She looked at him fully. She took all of him into her consciousness as though he was a newborn child. It was the only way she could look at him without wishing him dead. In this way, they began to see one another. After some time, they could look into each other's eyes and not flinch. They became friends. It's improbable but true. They became friends and she was rejected by many of her friends for it.

But the story doesn't end there. As the prisoner's parole date came near, he realised he had nowhere to live, no work to return to, no family or friends to rely on; he realised he was entirely alone in the world and that the person whose life he had torn apart was the only friend he had.

She took him in. She gave him her dead son's bedroom. She helped him find work and eventually she adopted him as her own son.

I can't even imagine the enormity of this woman's heart. Who behaves like this? Who amongst us has this much compassion or this much courage? Who amongst us knows how to truly love?

I'm not like this woman. I know your family deserted you after you were sentenced, but I've no intention of adopting you as my son. Besides, you're a grown man now, physically at least. The irony is, you've been like a son to me my whole life. I still have the small plate you gave me, the one with the dark blue flowers around the rim. There have been many times that I wanted to smash it, to hurl it across the kitchen and watch it shatter on the floor. But something always stopped me. We've known each other such a long time. Perhaps that gives us a head start?

I've discussed the logistics of taking you in as my carer with the appropriate legal and judicial bodies, and they've reluctantly agreed to grant early parole, as long as you accept my conditions (available as and when you decide to proceed). You will, of course, be on probation. Your signature below will set the wheels in motion.

You're an educated man, Quinn, for all the good it's done you. Perhaps you can find a way to respond.

Jennifer Holden

Let it be known that I have suffered. I read and reread the letters as though they were sacred texts, which, I suppose, they were. The only relief was that the pain in my arms, hands and penis had diminished. Greater torment came from the realisation that I had waited so long to open the envelope. In my stupidity, I had waited and ignored and forgotten. I had not chosen to allow the envelope into my memory. I had not chosen to gift it value. I could have opened this envelope many moons ago, and my own hand, my very own signature, could have put an end to this suffering. I had entrapped myself. My own foolishness had led to this prolonged incarceration, to the weariness and hunger that had eaten me for so long.

How was I to bear this new suffering?

20

Institutions and systems are laborious and craven, and so it took another twenty months before I was finally released from prison and delivered to Jennifer's house. I had ample time, therefore, to consider what it was she was asking of me.

Some of the maggots of my mind began to crawl away during that time. It was not because of anything I did or thought; it just happened. It was a kind of luck, I suppose, although I do not know whether I believe in luck. In any case, by the time I was escorted to see Anna about my release papers, Stone Man had gone.

'Tomás Quinn,' she said, although she was looking at the desk and not at me, 'you've to sign on the dotted line. Here.'

She pointed with a long nail that was painted purple, the colour of royalty.

'Yes,' I said.

I was glad that I did not have to face the crows again.

PART II

The sound of a woman praying

21

The house was almost as I remembered it. The front door had the same frosted-glass panel in the shape of a teardrop. The dark blue, almost black gloss paint was still peeling off the window frames. Farah's cherry blossom was perpetually in bloom next door and his small blonde mongrel sat beneath it like a statue.

Farah did not welcome me. It was some months before he would even glance at me from the box hedge enclave of his front garden. It did not surprise me.

'Got any new stories, Quinn?' he hissed through his brown-yellow smoker's teeth.

He had never been a friendly neighbour, even before my conviction and incarceration. He was the only man in the street who had not come over to visit the swan in our garden that strange winter. I had never set foot in his house and he had never set foot in ours. He never spoke to my parents or even acknowledged them as they passed his house. Perhaps my father was too bullish for Farah.

As Jennifer's body became more and more debilitated, so the areas of the house she occupied shrank. The downstairs had become her only living space, a kind of vault or cave in which the stench of illness hung. Her professional carers had set up a small corner of the living room as bedroom: bed, table, chair, bucket, clock. Above the bed was a small square window with a miniature dark blue blind. It opened on to the back garden and the fields beyond, where the foundations of a new housing estate had been abandoned. Tall grass had grown around the cement footings, so the fields resembled a series of disused bunkers or ancient sunken graves. You could not run there for fear of tripping. None of the dog walkers went there either, not even Farah.

The clock was particularly loud. It must have comforted Jennifer, or else why have such a monstrous reminder?

On the small bedside table, along with the clock, stood the paraphernalia of the dying: a neat row of bottled medicines, their labels facing forwards. I read the pharmaceutical information carefully, in the hope that I would understand what to administer if something out of the ordinary occurred. Yet everything was out of the ordinary.

Upstairs was my domain, Jennifer said, except that once a week she liked to bathe and so it was my duty to keep the bathroom spotless. Duty of care deemed that I did everything for Jennifer, except assist with the weekly bathe. For this, the professional carers continued to come to the house, and I was sent to my room for the duration of their visit.

This did not surprise me.

I learnt the language of mop and duster, hoover and washing machine, and became grateful for the machines in a way I had not experienced before. To wash the stench of terminal illness from the clothes of another by hand was unthinkable.

She had welcomed me on my arrival and I had not expected it. I had been delivered to her house like an unwanted parcel. Martin had taken it upon himself to be courier and I shook his hand before he left. It was not a firm shake. He was still wearing his dark blue uniform and the name tag that read 'M. Payne'.

Jennifer was in her wheelchair, and I could make out her silhouette on the other side of the frosted glass.

Five years passed, or the sun and the moon had tricked me, before Martin opened the door and she and I faced each other.

I had not expected friendliness, nor had I expected the way in which her face had aged. It had, of course, been some time since we had met, but her skin had lost its elasticity and colour, and the dark rings beneath her eyes made her appear more corpse than invalid. I was ashamed to see her face and experience it as ugly, repulsive even, and the task ahead began to feel insurmountable.

'Come in, Quinn. This isn't what you expected but come in anyway. The forecast is for rain.'

She had not lost her sense of humour, though it would be some months before she trusted me sufficiently to laugh. I was on probation after all. I was on a short leash, something Farah's dog was no doubt familiar with.

'Things have changed somewhat since you were last here.' She turned to me and paused. 'I'm glad you decided to come.'

The carpets had been ripped up and, in their place, mock wooden flooring had been laid. Her wheelchair rolled smoothly, the bright silver spokes of the wheels whirring round like the hands of a clock. Beneath the stench of illness, the toxic smell of flooring adhesive and plug-in air fresheners burnt the cilia of my nose.

Had I decided to come? Did I choose to exchange one insanity for another?

Something in me was shaking loose, a kind of expendable extra bone was rattling in me, making a small tapping sound in my chest. Every time I breathed I could hear its tap and after-tap, like the hands of a very large clock ticking. I felt untethered and yet this was not freedom. I had come to face with a woman I thought I knew, someone who had stitched a long, unbreakable thread between her life and mine. She was dying, that much was certain, but whose death would come first? My small extra bone tapped and ticked.

It was polite and perfunctory that first day. She gave me a tour of the downstairs from her wheelchair, and advised me to go upstairs and make sure there was everything that I needed.

What did I need?

The bedroom I was allocated was Andrea's old room. I entered the space without my limbs; at least, that is how it felt. My torso held me together, but my legs buckled and my arms flailed, and I found myself crumpled on the floor like a dog in the throes of death. The room was full of light. The curtains were drawn wide and the sunlight lit up the bed, desk, chair, bedside clock. Nothing was invisible. Nothing was hidden. Even the corners of the room shone with sunlight, and the small extra bone in my chest tapped and ticked as though it too had been exposed to this unbearable illumination.

On winter days when the rain was pouring and Jennifer had managed to persuade us – with milky tea and cake – not to go into the woods, Andrea would set an alarm to go off in one and a half minutes, and in this time we would assemble a den in her bedroom. Jennifer would give us old sheets and blankets, big cardboard boxes, anything that was useful for building secret spaces. I would have preferred to take my time and carefully lay out the boxes, blankets and sheets, tying the ends with string to the handles of the wardrobe, but Andrea always made us build in one and a half minutes flat. Whatever we had assembled by then, that was our castle. The truth is, it never was a joint effort: watching me build a den in one and a half minutes made her laugh so much that she was unable to help at all. In reality, she rolled on the floor in hysterics while I fumbled to build a castle that would be worthy of her. After one and a half minutes, the alarm would sound and she would jump up and stop me from making any further alterations. It was absurd, of course, but I always liked seeing her laugh. Tears would stream down her face and into her tea as we sat together, huddled inside a cardboard box with sheets drooping down on our heads.

It was on these rainy, cold afternoons that Andrea told me her best stories, inside our ramshackle castle. Even as a young girl, she was a good storyteller. In truth, she was much better at stories than I ever was. I never told her this and it took me many years to admit it to myself. There was one story that she told time and again, the one about the queen who made a cuckold of her king. Andrea liked the word 'cuckold' and I pretended to know what it meant.

As I stepped into the room that afternoon, it felt as though my body was not big enough to hold this memory intact. The same corners of the room looked back at me as on those innocent days of den building. The same wardrobe, the same patterned orange carpet that forgave every stain. My body could not hold the two opposite ends of the story at the same time. It was impossible, irreconcilable. How could this have been the story of my life with Andrea? If I built her a new castle, would she still love me after all that has happened, after all I have done?

For the first time in many years, I cried. I put my face in my hands and with the rough skin of my strange coat rubbing my chin, I cried for the suffering that had been and the suffering that was yet to come.

Five years passed, or the sun and the moon had tricked me. I heard Jennifer calling up the stairs, but I could not answer.

On Andrea's bed, the professional carers had laid out a large dark blue towel, a bar of lavender soap and a grey dressing gown. That I might wash myself clean. That the simple act of ablution might render me worthy.

22

There was an unravelling. This unravelling took the form of words and actions. Each day there was a further unravelling, until this body and this way of being in the world began to unremember itself. Words became like cut-glass vases. Actions became so necessarily slowed down that the body could accurately track each muscle extension. This was not welcome. I did not thrive. And yet, there was a softness that came into this space, something allowed and encouraged by Jennifer, that I had not experienced before. A softness that seemed to envelop both of us. I did not believe in this softness, but there it was, almost tangible.

23

The table was made of old pine and was narrow. I had no memory of it from previous years, perhaps because I had never been given the task of wiping it down and cleaning the crumbs out of the splits and knots. It was long enough that Jennifer could sit at it without the wheelchair knocking into the legs, and narrow enough that she could reach across from one side to the other; at least, for as long as her arms and hands remained mobile.

There was a hand-painted butter dish from Poland (probably a gift from my mother) and a pot of homemade strawberry jam, two plates, two knives, two cups, a dark blue teapot. Morning light was in the kitchen.

'I thought I would want to ask questions, Quinn, but now you're here, I don't. I don't want to waste time trying to understand what isn't understandable. It's not useful to me anymore.'

I stared at my plate, my hands in my lap. I did not want those words, as I knew they required the utmost patience of me, and it became clear, for the briefest moment, why I had been forced to become both master and servant of waiting. I knew how to wait. Nobody could tell me anything about waiting. It had become a deep art, a practice that I had been forcibly immersed in. It was like I had become waiting itself; I had stepped into the brick and cement clothing of waiting. It barely shifted on me and never creased. I could not be folded away neatly. Wait-bearer.

'This isn't about conviction or judgement,' she continued. 'This is a reckoning. And I don't mean a payback for the loss of Andrea. No, no.' She shook her head. 'It is far more than that.'

She pushed her cup towards the teapot and shakily poured. The tea was well stewed, almost black, and some of it pooled on the old pine table. I did not see her face, as the familiar pain and weariness were troubling my hands and neck, and I could scarcely breathe.

'Some people think I'm mad having you in my home. In fact, some people hate me for it, but I don't care anymore. It's too painful, too exhausting to keep insisting that it all add up! I've spent so much of my life measuring one thing against another and now I'm sick of it. It doesn't help. It never adds up.'

I could feel her eyes on me and managed a salutary nod. A money spider was making its way towards the butter dish in the middle of the table. It crawled fearlessly into the shadow cast by the jar of jam and continued on at the same pace. It was not unusual for me to kill spiders, but I did not move. The sun was pouring into the room.

'This isn't an act of disloyalty to Andrea. It's an act of freedom for myself – at least that's what I hope it is. I want to make peace with what I can't change. Do you understand?'

I did not understand but nodded. Some things are beyond the mind's understanding.

24

One autumn, Andrea and I erected a makeshift door out of an old wooden pallet that someone had dumped in the woods. The door did not work to make the den secret or hidden – which is always what dens are meant to be – because it was not solid and half of the cross-planks were missing or part broken. I took the pallet away without consulting her and she flew into a rage. I tried to explain my reasons and even showed her the alternative door I had found. I remember her white, angry face and the way her cheeks began to show those small red flecks like bright stars, just like my mother. She said she did not give a damn about the door; she was furious because I had gone ahead and made a decision without conferring with her.

I had measured everything to suit myself and it had not added up.

25

That very first morning with Jennifer stayed with me for months. There was loud birdsong and when I got up from the bed, I could see and feel the intensity of the sunlight through the glass window. I pushed the curtains as wide open as they would go. Blue tits, blackbirds, sparrows. I tried not to flinch from their rapid movement.

It was like the sun was burning out from my eyes into the world, as though my whole body were a vessel of light.

I looked at the clock: 6.00 a.m. There was time.

When I moved my body, I felt an unfamiliar gratitude, something open, or more open than I had experienced before. I did not know what it meant but it felt vulnerable, childish. I suppose it was relief, something I had not felt for years: one ordeal was over.

The landing and stairs were silent. Downstairs was silent. Jennifer would still be asleep, I thought, and I could explore the house at my leisure. Being able to walk between rooms, up and down stairs, was almost unbearable. Tears rose up to be swallowed. My throat held them tight.

This man's body. This sagging, torn-up, abandoned body.

Jennifer was more vulnerable than I was, of course. But that is not how it felt inside.

In the kitchen, she had a bright red electric kettle that my eye was repeatedly drawn to. It was the colour that attracted me, its depth and brightness. I had been deprived of red for so long.

I had not said sorry to her. The words felt wrong somehow, even ridiculous. I was sorry that she had experienced so much grief. I was sorry that she was slowly dying.

Jennifer called from her bed in the living room and I walked in to the first day of caring.

She knew how cut off I was, but she worked with me anyway.

After that, there was red everywhere: robins, peonies, blistered hands, blood.

26

The diagnosis of Jennifer's illness was made in the year that Andrea turned fourteen, so I would have been fifteen. It changed everything. Andrea began to withdraw into herself, to become quiet in a way I had not experienced her before. In the early days of Jennifer's illness, she skipped school for many months and then left as soon as she was legally allowed to. I remember the disappointment of the teaching staff, to see such a bright girl throw everything away to care for her mother. But they did not understand the way Andrea loved. Even I, and perhaps even Jennifer, did not understand the way she loved. The fierceness of her heart was a rare thing. Everyone else I knew had built a fine suit of armour around their heart, armour that was so good at its job that the organ inside began to wither. Nothing got in and nothing got out. Only Andrea let her heart be open to the world, even to its injustice and suffering.

This was a time of enduring pain for both our families, as we came to accept the terminal illness of Jennifer and my brother. It was a struggle. It was a struggle which Andrea rose to and I sank beneath. We had known about my brother's illness for many years, but Jennifer's diagnosis somehow deepened our own tragic predicament. At least, that is how it seemed to me. I could not conjure the kind of comfort that Andrea seemed to find in the most unlikely places.

She and I would see each other on the street or at school but would barely speak or even make eye contact. She withdrew from me. I watched her study the small things of the earth – the beetles and dandelions and single blades of grass. It was as though this attention to detail held her intact, safe somehow, as though this attention shrank the severity of her difficult life. Sometimes she had an air of sadness about her, but never one of resignation and rarely one of anger.

I had to wait many months before she returned to me, and when she did, she had changed. She seemed to have grown up beyond her years. I suppose the pain of living alongside death does that to people whose hearts are open. The certainty of death takes time to get used to, and sometimes there is not enough room inside one person's body to also accommodate other people's demands and needs. 'It all depends on the heart,' she said to me.

Andrea and her mother were very close and adored each other. It is not a lie to say that I was envious of their relationship.

'Please make me two eggs, Quinn. I'm hungrier than usual this evening.' I found the small plate with dark blue flowers around the rim to serve the eggs on.

27

The morning was not fresh, but I pushed Jennifer out none-theless. A part of me had dreaded being seen outside, but it was in fact a relief to leave the claustrophobia of the house and to walk the streets of the housing estate. The air was cloying but did not carry the stench of illness or death. Instead, exhaust fumes, burnt cooking oil and dog shit. There were no parks nearby, only the woods at the far end of the street, but neither Jennifer nor I wanted to go there, and besides, the woodland paths were not suitable for a wheelchair. Apart from the woods and Farah's pink cherry blossom, it was a grey concrete world: grey walls, grey pavement, grey houses, grey lawns. Even the windows reflected back grey, and the sky was a grey rag that nobody had ever washed. The wheels of her chair turned smoothly, the silver spokes ticking.

I was safe because of Jennifer. Every house hated me. Every lamp post and gutter. It would have been simple to stab me dead, but nobody dared to take Jennifer's carer away. My small extra bone tapped and ticked.

Farah's cherry blossom was in full bloom, and he was standing in his garden, smoking, the same as every morning. He waved at Jennifer, and his blonde mongrel looked but did not bark. He was a disagreeable man, a bigot, who had no education to speak of. He would often ask what Jennifer was reading, and then nod knowledgeably and speak highly of the author. Jennifer humoured him.

'Got any new stories, Quinn?' he hissed through his brown-yellow smoker's teeth.

28

I was sleepless for many weeks. I suffered greatly. Andrea's room was never dark, even though the curtains were heavy and the nights often cloudy. I would lie awake staring at the walls and ceiling as though I were back in my cell. The wardrobe had mirrored double doors, which reflected every remnant light wave, and when the nights were clear, the moon shone in like a searchlight.

The weariness and hunger that had been my constant companions did not let up. And now, alongside these, there was rage. Sometimes there was so much rage, I feared for my life. I could not settle it. I could not order it. There was no obvious reason for its presence, and the confusion it created only served to feed it further. This was exacerbated, no doubt, by the insomnia, and by the fact that there was no outlet for it; clearly, I could not rage at Jennifer.

As the days lengthened into weeks, I became aware of a gradual numbing. I spent each day attending to the needs of Jennifer and each night lying awake in torment. My senses began to switch off, as though they could not bear the enormity of the transition from prison cell to this new, wayward kind of freedom. I did not know where to turn. Jennifer watched me like a hawk, and I had to pay the utmost attention to my words and actions in order to pass muster.

Something had to give.

29

That my own father beat me was a recurrent shock. I do not know why, but in the early years of my life I never expected or anticipated his brutality. It was as though a part of me so wholly disbelieved it, that each successive beating was like the first. There was one occasion, however, when something shifted in me. I was nine years old. My body rebelled and would not let me forget.

I had missed the school bus that afternoon, and so I had to walk the five miles back home. I was very happy about it. I remember skipping along the roads and back alleys that led to our house, the route my brother and I would take in the summer if he was well enough. That afternoon was especially exciting because it was winter and already dusk. I could easily make out my body and the surroundings as I set out, but as time ticked on, everything became blurred and fuzzy, and then darkness fell. Of course, there were streetlamps that lit the way, or most of the way, but otherwise I walked in darkness. To walk five miles in the dark on my own was a delicious risk and thrill.

I remember passing the yard where the Shaws kept their gloomy-looking ponies. I always particularly liked the white one, probably because she was never clean and white to look at, but I knew that underneath she was. The Shaw man who owned them was out in the yard giving the ponies some feed. He waved at me but I did not wave back.

'Heya!' He gestured to me with his head, nodding it up and back like a horse. 'How yer doin'? D'you wanna feed 'er?'

I did not know whether to stop or not. I wanted to, but I was afraid. I looked down and saw that my school shoes were covered in mud, and so it would not matter if they got even more muddy or coated in horse shit. Besides, I liked the smell of horse shit – it reminded me of all animals.

As a child, it always seemed to me that animals knew how to discern safety from danger, right from wrong, yes from no. It was not true, of course, but I believed that they inhabited a kind of ease and freedom that was unfamiliar to me. When I look back now, I realise that what they gave me was hope.

'Sure,' I said, but I was not.

I walked around the side of the smelly yard, past the small, rotting wooden stable where the ponies sometimes sheltered from the wind and rain. It was made with a light brown wood, probably pine, but in the dusk, it looked dark and sombre.

The Shaw man appeared suddenly from around the side of the stable and startled me.

He laughed softly, 'Yer alright! C'mon!' and led me by the arm to the ponies.

There were three in total, two dark ones and the white pony that was grey with mud and shit and whatever pollution from the roads had stuck to her. She was neither fat nor thin and had a long grey mane that she swished about while she chewed the hay. I knew she was a girl because the other two ponies had penises, and sometimes when I drove past in the school bus, the children would roar with laughter and point and jeer if one of the boy ponies had an erection.

'I've apples,' the Shaw man said. 'D'you wanna give 'er un?'

I held the apple flat in my palm, like the Shaw man showed me. By that time it was pitch dark, but the yard was lit with one of those lights that switches on and off when there is movement. On windy days, it flashed all the time. I had watched the ponies for years and I knew the shape of their faces, the long line of their jaws. I knew the way they stood in the yard and in what order at the feeding station. I knew which pony got to the cradle of hay first – the mare – and which one preferred oranges to apples – the mare.

If I had grown up in a different family in a different country or in a more rural setting, perhaps I would have grown up to be a horseman. Perhaps I would have learnt to ride and jump horses. Perhaps being with the animals every day – caring for them, mucking them out, feeding and watering them – would have softened something in me. Andrea and I could have lived together on a farm with ponies and horses. They would have grazed the meadows and wandered in the woods.

Andrea had a favourite book from her childhood that was about a horse and an ox who became lifelong friends. The story told of the difficulties the animals encountered – the usual parable of the unhappy and neglectful owner – and it told of the stark differences in temperament of the two ungulates; of their gradual acceptance of each other's unique way of being in the world. They were both powerful creatures, of course, but the horse had a form of grace and nobility in its bearing that the ox only knew through graft. To be noble, the ox had to work, to shift its bulk over the earth, whereas the horse need only stand looking out to sea. The ox was slow and heavy, the horse lithe and so fast that the illustrator sometimes chose to show only its back end, tail flying out in the wind, as it sped away across the fields. It made the pages of the book look ill cut, but the child need only turn the page and there was the full body of the horse, grinning. The ox was far from stupid, but it failed to see that it was not meant to be a horse. Its role was to plough the fields and to shift weight and mass from one place to another. It was very good at this, at little cost to itself: the heart was clean enough, the bones strong enough, the flesh willing enough to lean into the task.

It was an obvious, clichéd story, but I saw how much it meant to Andrea and I managed to keep my mouth shut. It was a rare act of generosity on my part.

Feeding the white pony that was not white was a moment that stayed with me for a long time. In fact, it is not a lie to say that the moment has stayed with me all my life.

The soft but bristly lip of the pony's muzzle in my palm tickled and delighted me. It was warm and felt like life. Her breath was sweet, grassy, even though she lived in a concrete yard and probably never knew what it was like to run in fields of long grass. It was only brief, the contact between the pony's mouth and my palm, but it was long enough for me to feel something like love. She expected nothing of me, unless I had oranges to give her.

From that afternoon on, I would always wave at the ponies from the school bus as we passed, and occasionally the Shaw man would be there too and would wave back. Until the day one of the boys in my class called me a soppy baby and the whole bus laughed.

When I finally got home, I was many hours late and my parents were afraid. I remember seeing my mother's pale cheeks and worried eyes, and I remember wishing she was a pony instead. If only I could remedy everything with oranges and apples.

My father hit me repeatedly with the buckle end of his belt. Mostly, he hit the back of my legs and my backside, but he also hit me across the chest and one of the strikes caught my chin. I remember my mother crying out because the snib of the buckle broke my skin and I bled on the living-room carpet.

A day later, as my mother was tending the wound, she said, 'What did I say to you about the winnowing fan! Do you never listen? Winnowing fan!' She repeated these two words over and over, as though they were somehow going to heal me. The term was taken from the Gospel of Matthew, and of course I can still remember the whole verse:

> His winnowing fan is in His hand, and He will thoroughly clean out His threshing floor, and gather His wheat into the barn; but He will burn up the chaff with unquench-able fire.

As I understand it, the winnowing fan is an encouragement to be discerning, but my mother used it as a reprimand. She would often scold me with this biblical quote when something in my life went wrong, something she clearly thought I could have avoided had I been more discerning. It was her way of trying to teach me to toe the line, to behave impeccably in order to limit the damage my father inflicted. Of course, it never worked and her warped perspective had nothing to do with true discernment – in any case, it was not possible to discern the right action when it came to dealing with my father. I suppose in her eyes, controlling me was an act of salvation. When I think about it now, I realise that she was the least discerning person I have known. I think she needed to ram the winnowing fan down her own throat.

Some years later, after I was sentenced, my parents moved away from the street, and I have seen neither of them since. I thought my mother might visit me, but she never did. Perhaps it was too painful for her. Perhaps she was too ashamed of me. I waited for many years but she did not come. Even on the day of my release to Jennifer's, I hoped she might be at the gate to embrace me, to welcome me back into the outside world. But it was not the case.

She had become a ghost, as all the people in my life become eventually. I could barely recall her face. She seemed to belong to a life that was not mine. I wish I had been able to give up waiting, to give up hoping. It would have made the early years of incarceration easier. On one level, I would have been free.

Nobody moved in to replace my parents and the house stood empty and neglected. A part of me was glad.

30

It is important not to believe everything you read or hear spoken of. I learnt this well as a child – the misuse of Bible quotes for one. But some things stay with you, whether they are true or not, whether they are valuable or not. Can I unlearn what my mother drilled into me?

I believed that because my father came from Ireland, he did not know how to be sober. I believed that because my mother came from Poland, she did not know how to be discerning. But I was wrong on both counts. Place has nothing to do with the human soul, even though people like to think it does. Place impregnates the personality, but that does not mean we have no choice about our actions.

I did not want this to be true. I fought it many, many times.

31

Balram Farah had grown up in Portugal. He was Indian. At least, his parents and grandparents were Indian and so he was brought up as an Indian in Portugal. He had grey skin and smelt of curry. He wore dark blue nylon slacks and ill-fitting polyester pullovers.

Some months after my release, he invited Jennifer to his house for a cup of tea. It was quite out of character and both Jennifer and I were surprised. Or perhaps it is more honest to say that Jennifer was surprised and I was suspicious. I did not want to go, but there was no choice – someone had to wheel the chair up his driveway. I suppose Farah wanted to glower at me and confirm his vicious prejudice. I barely spoke, but Farah did not address a single comment to me either. It did not matter. Besides, the dog was far more interesting, and the furnishings.

His front room was busy with bamboo wallpaper and chintzy dark blue curtains, as though he were a lonely, suburban panda. He was not married and I never found out whether he had been or whether he had children. But I knew Farah would have talked long and hard about his children and grandchildren if he had had any.

'Yes, Portugal, in the mountains, near a city called Coimbra. Very hot in the summer and lots of peasant farmers. My parents were entrepreneurs, and my grandparents were entrepreneurs, so they knew how to work and make a success of their lives, and I suppose the climate wasn't all that different from Goa.'

I wanted to ask him whether he was an entrepreneur, but how could he be? He had ended up in dreary suburbia, after such a promising upbringing in Portugal. There were many things I wanted to ask him but did not.

'Must have been nice growing up there,' Jennifer said, lifting a china teacup to her lips.

The room smelt of mouldy carpet and dog. Farah's small blonde mongrel was silent. It did not even bark when the postman came to the door. It was rotund like its owner and always sought out the patch of sun in the room. As we sat and drank endless cups of tea, the strip of sunlight on the carpet moved west and so the dog moved west. I forgot to ask its name. I remember its peace and the way its body seemed to glow in the heat and sunlight. It was like a living battery, absorbing the energy of the sun in order to keep on worshipping it. Its eyes were mostly closed, but when it did look at you, it saw all the ways in which you had failed.

'Yes, yes,' he said, 'my parents left Goa in the late sixties, bringing me and my grandparents with them. We all moved together, the whole family, with all the siblings and all our possessions. It must have been expensive and quite a risk really – to start all over again in a new country. But they were entrepreneurs, you see. They knew how to build and rebuild lives.'

'How old were you then?'

'Quite young, Mrs Holden, about ten, maybe.' He stroked his chin and mouth in contemplation. 'Yes, that's about right. A long time ago now.'

'We've been neighbours so long now, do call me Jennifer.'

'Ah, Jennifer, yes, a beautiful name.'

'I've been thinking that it would be nice to have a pond in our back garden. Quite a large one, so that we could keep ducks. Do you eat duck eggs at all?' But she didn't wait for him to reply. 'I wanted to let you know my plans, as there'll likely be some noisy and lengthy digging, and, well, are you OK with ducks?'

Farah did not look pleased but he nodded and made encouraging noises.

'My only concern is that my dog doesn't like the water. In fact she can't swim. She's lame and a bulldog cross – not a good breed for swimming.'

The dog opened its eyes and yawned. The sun had gone behind a cloud.

'Then I'll make sure to repair the fence between our two houses,' Jennifer said, smiling. She took another sip of tea and thanked him.

32

You cannot kill two birds with one stone.

A high wind came the day I began digging the pond, and it did not let up for a week. The air pushed into my lungs and brain. I felt light-headed, dizzy, and had to sit down more than once. My body was not used to so much oxygen and open space. The garden felt enormous. I could stretch out my arms and legs as wide as possible, and still have room for ten other men to stretch alongside me. The pain in my lower back subsided momentarily.

When the wind blew like this, the tall grass in the back field swished and ticked around the footings. My eyes could see a long way. Things have been done that hurt the mouth to speak of.

I used bamboo canes to mark out the shape, tying string between each one. It was rough and I did not know what I was doing. Jennifer watched from the back door. She told me she did not care what shape the pond was, as long as it was not exacting. She did not want something formal with neat paving slabs at the edges.

I was to remove the turf first, slicing into the lawn with the sharp edge of the spade and then lifting the surface inches as though I were cutting peat. It was slow work, especially with a body that had not exerted itself physically for so long. My limbs felt weak, wobbly, my former strength drained. It was an assault on my muscles to dig, slice, bend, lift, turn.

Over the course of the first week, during the snatched hours when I was able to leave Jennifer in her wheelchair or resting in her bed, I cleared a large kidney-bean patch of ground and stacked the turfs by the fence. The brown earth was like an open wound.

If I could speak clearly, answers would come. What am I doing? What is this fragile body now?

I bent low to begin excavating the shape and felt a sharp tug in my lower back. I bent low to dig anyway. I felt the pull of the deep earth and the need to dig out the shape. This shape was for Andrea as much as for Jennifer, and my body wanted the digging in spite of the pain.

I cannot speak of this pain. There are no words wide enough or deep enough to capture it. Let it be known that I have suffered. Let it be known that the rage in me was a scatter bomb, that the spade could have easily removed both my feet.

An erasure of doing and deeds and done.

Are you done for the day, Quinn? What did you do out there?

The woods were darker than I remembered and dense. Daylight had not yet fully penetrated the crisscross of branches and the place felt inert, more plantation than woodland. Birds were calling — tits, wood pigeons — and everything was wet from recent rain. As I stepped forwards, mud and leaves reluctantly let go of my boots. There was something erotic about it.

I understood about mud and reluctance and rain.

I headed straight for the silver birch, our tree. The sun was beginning to shine between clouds, and the bark glowed. One white incisor in a forest of teeth — that's what Andrea called it. She was bound to be somewhere near here. This was where we met on Fridays, after she had finished with her mother and I had completed the week's story. A single silver birch in the middle of larch and pine, and the big car-wash brushes of spruce.

Let it be known that I have suffered.

I dug for three hours without stopping and my back was raw. I had forgotten the time. Jennifer would need help with lunch. Bread, cheese, the simple things. Eggs.

I looked at my hands: red, with blisters forming at the base of my fingers where the hand exerts pressure, works with the tool. My fingers stayed in a claw-like position for some minutes after I put the spade down. The body remembers everything.

It did not matter that my muscles ached and complained. The pain kept me in my body. I could not run away. Lifting Jennifer, even though she was bird-like, sent shooting pains up my spine and down my legs into my toes. I bore the pain silently. Perhaps this was a kind of reckoning.

33

I dreamt I had made a mistake. From the Old Norse *mistaka*, to take in error.

I was travelling on a high-speed train at night. A woman in a dark blue overcoat, old enough to be a mother, went into the toilet. She was in there a good ten minutes before I heard her calling. Evidently, she was trying to push the button to get out, but the door remained locked. For some time, she continued to press the button, as though it was possible she had got the angle wrong or the pressure, but the truth was, the door mechanism had broken. It was obvious that the connector that operated the door had snapped or shorted, and she was stuck inside. She started banging on the door and yelling. She must have known that I was the only person in the carriage. I waited. She was not in danger; she was not going to die in there.

After a while, I got up and walked over to the toilet door, leant against it.

'OK,' I said, 'let me find someone to get you out. If you can wait just a few more minutes, I promise to come back.'

But I did not go back. I left the carriage and walked away.

In error, I took something from her and something from myself.

34

You cannot kill two birds with one stone.

The digging was lengthy, Jennifer had been right. It was not one week's work or two. It was several weeks before the pond was deep enough to begin thinking about fitting a liner.

Farah walked up to the gap in the fence with his lame dog and tutted loudly.

'The repair?' he bawled.

His dog hobbled. I felt sorry for it.

The earth was sandy, alluvial, for which I was grateful. The deeper I dug, the stronger the smell of river, of cold water. It was like digging down through time, clearing away the debris of history. I felt archaeological. After the initial weeks of blisters and muscle pain, my arms and hands became strong again. My back, though, still troubled me.

The rage did not leave me, but I used it to dig. The fierceness of my emotion dug the pond, and on the final day of digging, I got in and lay down. There were still piles of soil around the edge, high enough to create a kind of bunker and sound chamber that might contain my rage. I lay face down in the hole and howled into the earth.

When I find her, they will have to eat their words.

But there would be no finding. The taste of earth was in my mouth. I could sense the river that must once have flowed here, as though it were my own life force. My small extra bone tapped and ticked.

There was shame in me that could not be held in one hand nor in one hundred.

I did not want this strange coat anymore, nor these endlessly muddy boots. I took Andrea's doll out of my pocket, tried to wipe the mud from its face with my muddy hands. The mud was all over me, in my nostrils and fingernails and hair.

35

It is not for me to say what any of this means. I am caught between suffering and surviving, and I cannot imagine it to be otherwise. All I know is that once the pond had been lined and filled, and the wire fence between Jennifer's garden and Farah's repaired, a series of events took place that unravelled every story ever told about injustice. It was as though a violent curse landed with the ducks on the pond.

The pond was an eyesore for some time, until the ferns and bulrushes I planted grew and softened the outline. I never liked it, even then, but Jennifer was determined to keep ducks, not just for their eggs but because they gave her something to delight in – the softness of their feathers, their coloured bills and webbed feet. She chose a mixed flock of mallards and white Campbells, three drakes and ten female ducks. They would be good layers, she said, and unlikely to fly off.

There was something false about the pond, as though everyone knew the old river should have been there instead.

Farah did not like it either. He took to standing at the fence with the dog for his morning smoke, his mouth and eyes set like a statue's. He never conversed with me and I did my best to ignore him, busying myself with feeding the ducks and hosing down the patio.

Over time, the ducks became more courageous and pluckier. The drakes in particular would waddle right up to the fence where Farah and his dog were, and hiss or *peep*. It was the only time I heard the dog bark. Farah would scold her and the ducks with words that did not sound English.

It was not unusual for me to feel the weight of Farah's loathing on my back. There was something intimate and controlling about it that oppressed me. He would not let me be anything other than what he thought I was: inhuman, lesser. I could cross and recross one million roads to help the old woman or the injured child, and he would still hate me with righteous fury. Still this unspoken anger would drip from his stale tongue into the silent, waiting pond.

36

The ducks were not an altogether peaceable flock. In fact it was the drakes who were the troublemakers, although that did not become apparent until after the carnage.

I knew nothing about keeping ducks and was not prepared for the fallout. Jennifer too had been naive. She had not prepared sufficiently for keeping ducks, and so what happened was not surprising.

The night of the slaughter, I heard nothing. My room was at the front of the house and for once I had slept all night. As I got up out of bed, my small extra bone tapped and ticked.

The lawn and pond were strewn with white feathers, and the patio was smeared with blood. At least three of the ducks were dead, their limp bodies abandoned on the grass. I did not care for the birds anyway; their beaks and wings were a menace to me, and now I would have to clean up the mess.

'Quinn?'

'Yes.'

It must have been a fox. What other animal kills more than it needs to survive?

37

I opened the back door and walked out. The three drakes flapped towards me, quacking, and I counted six ducks, most of them huddled in the far corner of the garden beneath the lilac. Three bodies. The fox had taken one duck.

I gathered the dead birds and laid them on one of the paving slabs, covered them with a plastic sack. The morning was cloudy and it had started to rain. In my hands, their limpness felt inexplicable. Their necks were rangy and blood smeared.

I had left the back door open and could hear Jennifer calling from the living room.

'OK!' I yelled.

I did not want to gather up the feathers. Much of the loose down was soggy with rain and it stuck to my fingers. There was something ugly about the pond with so many feathers floating in it, and I did not like to look.

'Quinn! Come here immediately! Please!'

I threw the remainder of the flock some corn and went inside to Jennifer.

'Well?'

I looked at her indignant face and knew, in that brief moment, that I would never understand the depth of frustration she must feel. It is one thing to be locked away by another, and something else altogether to be locked away by one's own body.

'A fox,' I said. 'Four dead.'

'It's my fault,' Jennifer said.

She gestured for me to help her into her wheelchair, and I pushed her through to the kitchen. She looked at the plastic sack on the paving slab. One of the ducks' bills was still visible. I could see that she was close to tears.

'Quinn, we must build a duck house, so they have somewhere to go that's safe.'

She looked up at me with tears on her cheeks.

'I'm so sorry,' she said, 'this is all my fault. I should've been more aware.'

My small extra bone tapped and ticked.

38

She was no longer a young woman, but neither was she old. I had helped her to dress and undress dozens of times already, but that morning was different. Something left my body, and I cannot name it. It was something dark blue, almost black, and it flew from me like a huge bird. I knew it would not be back, and I was glad.

Her arms were so thin they could have been snapped like two dry sticks. Small, soft flaps of skin were beginning to hang from the underside of her upper arms as the muscles wasted and her strength diminished.

She did not hide herself from me. There was no shame, at least not on her part. It took me many months of caring for her to become comfortable with the routine of dressing and undressing. It did not arouse me, but there was something about it that made me feel vulnerable and I did not like it.

Her empty, drooping breasts hung down, since they had no further work to do. She would joke lovingly about her breasts, as though they had always been her good friends. I did not know how to respond, but as the months went on, I took to smiling and nodding as she jested. This body of hers began also to be my friend, someone I got to know quite well, even though I was not permitted the intimacy of bathing her.

There was something powerful in her body that I had never witnessed before and could not have articulated back then: not the beauty of youth and ample shapeliness, but the bone and flesh power of an aging body that knew its intrinsic worth and magnificence. I still cannot explain what I mean, but this truth that Jennifer embodied has stayed with me, on and on.

Sometimes she would be bashful, as though she had returned in those moments to a younger woman, to a body that knew its own allure and delighted in it. Then she would catch my eye and the moment would pass, unspoken.

She was a bright, courageous woman. She knew what she was doing.

I, on the other hand, was a fool, an imbecile, who took so very long to learn anything. It took me several years to accept this fact alone.

She chose to wear a red dress that day, with small white birds flying across the material in a repeat pattern. It was the kind of dress a young girl would wear to a birthday party. I made her a cup of tea in a red cup, using the red electric kettle to boil the water. I told Jennifer that I liked seeing her in red, that it suited her. She smiled.

'Let's go out and buy you a new coat, Quinn,' she said. 'That old one's really seen better days.'

She did not say it like a parent. She said it like a friend, and it took all my inner strength not to cry. I thanked her. I did not want to wear the strange coat anymore. The fabric was too coarse for a coat. It was like rough, hairy skin, and whenever the rain beat down, it became slippery.

39

The trouble with the drakes began shortly after the slaughter. The fox did not return, and even if it had, I had made the ducks safe in a run and spent time building a house for them to retreat to at night. I no longer needed to hunt for their eggs, which was a good thing, as it took time and I could never tell how fresh the eggs were, especially if I found some in a new nesting spot.

The house solved all that, but now we had three drakes and only six ducks. As the mating season came around, the drakes became more and more aggressive. I did not know that there was such a thing as over-mating in the animal kingdom. I did not know that the ducks needed protecting from the over-aggressive drakes. I did not know that drakes tend to claim territory of a certain number of females, and that if this was not possible, the females would be fought over, sometimes to the death of both the opponent drakes and the ducks. The aggressive drakes would mount any member of the flock, pecking the feathers from the back of the bird's neck and forcing the females into repeated mating sessions. Sometimes, all three drakes would mount one female, fighting over her, Jennifer said, as though she was an object to be owned or won in battle. If this happened on the pond, the duck would invariably drown, unless I managed to get to the drakes in time. I don't know why I bothered. This was nature doing what it does, after all. I was interfering with the natural order of things.

Perhaps I did it to appease Jennifer.

Very soon, the flock declined. By the end of the first year, we had lost a total of one drake and seven ducks. There was nothing bucolic about keeping these birds in the back garden. I had not cared for them from the start, and now I was even less interested in their welfare.

Jennifer, on the other hand, stepped up her involvement and saw to it that I became closely engaged in and observant of the remaining flock's behaviour. She bought books and together we read at the kitchen table, finally working out what combination of ducks and drakes was most likely to result in a harmonious flock. Having too many drakes in a small flock was not recommended.

Farah would stand at the fence with his dog and sneer at our ineptitude.

'A high mortality rate, Quinn.'

He never looked at me when he spoke, preferring instead to study his cigarette or some hangnail he repeatedly tugged at. The white Campbell drake would rush over and hiss aggressively at them both. The dog would become aggressive in return, barking and lunging towards the bird from the other side of the wire fence. I think this was the point at which I began to feel an affinity for the bird.

I am not ashamed to say that they got what was coming to them, Farah and his dog.

40

Things have been done that hurt the mouth to speak of.

This is not what I have chosen, and this *is* what I have chosen. I cannot speak easily of Andrea, but I can speak of Farah and his dog. It was not my fault that the dog drowned in the pond. It was inevitable. All stories lead in the direction they must go in. Once a tale has begun, it has its own momentum and its own desire. There is very little choice for the characters, whether they are human or not. Whereas in real life, Jennifer said, there is agency.

Farah was up especially early looking for his dog. He was heard calling, then yelling, then panicking in his garden, shortly after dawn. Evidently, the dog was nowhere to be found. The name he was calling did not sound English.

I got up and went downstairs to the kitchen. Farah was pacing up and down the grass on the other side of the wire fence.

He was still wearing his dressing gown and his thinning hair was in disarray.

Jennifer had called me, so I went to help her. Instead of getting her dressed straightaway, she asked for her pale blue shawl, so that she could be wheeled out to see what all the fuss was. Farah was still bawling.

One end of the shawl got caught momentarily in the spokes of the wheelchair, and it took me a few minutes to unravel it and push her through to the kitchen unimpeded. It seemed to me that she was getting lighter and less substantial every day.

The dog was floating face down in the pond. It was several minutes before either of us noticed it, as we were both looking across at Farah, wondering what to do – Jennifer wanted to help, but I did not. When we saw the dog, she gasped. The animal looked very small in the water. Much of its body was submerged, I suppose. What remained visible was the dark blonde ruff of its neck, darker than usual because of the water.

'Quinn, get it out! Quickly, get it out!'

She gestured towards the door, but I did not move. I knew how these things got played out. I did not want Farah's wrath and blame. It seemed to rise up before me like a hot-air balloon.

'It has nothing to do with me,' I said.

But as soon as I said those words, I realised I had set my own fate, and there was only one course of action open to me, only one choice. Reluctantly, I opened the back door and walked outside to the pond. Farah had gone around the other side of his house, but I could still hear him yelling for his dog.

I got a stick and poked the body over towards me, so that I could lift it out. Its eyes were still open, those deep, dark brown pools, and the folds of skin on its face and muzzle were puckered and greasy-looking. It must not have been a good death.

Jennifer had pulled the tea towel from the hook by the sink and was waiting in her chair at the back door. She took the dog from me and wrapped it in the towel like a baby. She swaddled it and rubbed its body dry.

'You have to take it round to Mr Farah,' she said.

I had never seen such fierceness in her as I saw that day. She would not let me off the hook. She insisted that I do all the things that I did not want to do. I was to rescue the dog. I was to return the body to Farah. I was to receive the loathing and righteous anger of the man who loved this animal.

She looked me in the eye and I knew there was no choice. She had offered me so much, and now I was to do this for her and for Farah, a man I hated as much as he hated me. She lifted the dog from her lap and held it out to me. It looked ridiculous, wrapped in a tea towel with its dead face peeking out. Jennifer said a prayer over the body and I suppressed a smirk. I had not hated the dog. I did not hate the dog now, but I was glad that Farah would suffer.

Let it be known that I have suffered.

The man was distraught in a way I had not witnessed before. As Farah saw me walking up the driveway with the bundle in my arms, his face collapsed in on itself. An animal in shock, with a body that was not big enough to bear the trauma.

A muffled cry came from his mouth as he rushed towards me and took the dead dog from my arms. He fell to his knees, clutching the animal and sobbing into its cold, wet face.

I stood there. The morning air was pleasant, and for the first time, I was glad of Farah's pink cherry blossom.

He jerked his head up at me, his eyes wide with fury.

'You bastard!' he said. 'I hope you rot in hell!'

His dressing gown flapped open as he stood up, and I saw that he was wearing no underpants. This has stayed with me, not because I found it erotic – on the contrary – but because the proximity of the dead dog and Farah's shrivelled genitalia elicited a feeling of vulnerability in me that I had not experienced before. I did not like it. I turned and walked back into Jennifer's house.

Later that day, we watched as Farah dug a hole in his back garden and buried the dog. Jennifer had instructed me to make enough dinner for the three of us, so that we could offer Farah the comfort of a meal. I did not tell her what he had said to me, and I did not tell her how I wished to put laburnum seeds in his portion of the meal.

He stood at the graveside with his head bowed and his hand on the spade. The day had stayed dry and the ducks were swimming happily on the pond.

'You must take the food to him, Quinn. He won't want to socialise tonight.'

'You will have to come with me, then.'

She looked puzzled but nodded. I helped her into her woollen cardigan.

'I'd like to offer him my condolences anyway,' she said.

The house was quiet and unlit. The front door had the same frosted-glass panel in the shape of a teardrop. Dark blue, almost black gloss paint was peeling off the window frames. I pushed Jennifer up the driveway and rang the doorbell. There was no reply. I rang again.

Five years passed, or the sun and the moon had tricked me, before Farah opened the door and we all faced each other.

I had not expected friendliness and did not receive it; nor had I expected the way in which his face had aged.

'Mr Farah, I'm so sorry for your loss.'

Farah raised his gaze to Jennifer. His eyes were puffy and red from crying, and he did not respond for some time. We stood in awkward silence on the threshold. He was not going to invite us inside, and I was glad.

'We've brought you a small gift – just a meal to warm your belly,' Jennifer said. 'Perhaps you can put it in the fridge if you don't feel hungry tonight.'

Jennifer passed the dish to Farah, a small white bowl with a tinfoil lid.

He did not say thank you.

'You're housing an evil man,' he spat, not even looking at me. 'You ought to be ashamed of yourself, Mrs Holden.'

In the weeks and months that followed, I recalled the dog's peace, and the way its body seemed to glow in the heat and sunlight that day in Farah's house. It was like a living battery, absorbing the energy of the sun in order to keep on worshipping it. I still did not know its name and now I never would.

41

It is not possible to believe that Farah had the strength and the wherewithal to single-handedly fill in the pond. It happened overnight and in silence – neither Jennifer nor I heard a thing – as though the fairies had come and done the deed.

An extension of doing and deeds and done.

It was a very precise deed. The fairies had come at a liminal hour, removed the ferns and bulrushes, drained the pond of water, refilled it with earth and replaced the turfs as though they had never been removed. The garden travelled back in time. It shed many years, and with those years went not only the pond but also the ducks and duck house, as well as the repaired section of fence between Jennifer's house and Farah's.

Jennifer was as baffled as I.

'Is this your doing, Quinn? What did you do out there?'

*The woods were darker than I remembered and dense. Daylight
had not yet fully penetrated the crisscross of branches and the place
felt inert, more plantation than woodland. Birds were calling –
tits, wood pigeons – and everything was wet from recent rain.
As I stepped forwards, mud and leaves reluctantly let go of my
boots. There was something erotic about it.*

I understood about mud and reluctance and rain.

*I headed straight for the silver birch, our tree. The sun was begin-
ning to shine between clouds, and the bark glowed. One white
incisor in a forest of teeth – that's what Andrea called it. She
was bound to be somewhere near here. This was where we met
on Fridays, after she had finished with her mother and I had
completed the week's story. A single silver birch in the middle of
larch and pine, and the big car-wash brushes of spruce.*

I walked into the garden to the place where the pond used
to be. There was no sign that it had ever existed. There were
no marks in the turf, and the turf itself was unimpaired
and thriving. I searched in all the old places that the ducks
used to lay before I built them their house, but there were
no eggs and no signs that the birds had been there. At the
back of the garden, where the fence marked out Jennifer's
property from the fields that stretched out beyond, I found

a single duck feather and put it in my pocket together with Andrea's doll.

We did not speak of the pond again and Farah never said a word either. He did not comment on the reappearance of the gap in the fence, and he did not stand on early mornings in his garden smoking. I rarely saw him, and whenever I did, he would turn his back to me and I would feel the hatred travel from his body towards mine. It was as though the intensity of his hate for me became manifest in a palpable energetic form. It was dark blue, almost black.

42

I never believed in forgiveness. I never thought it was possible to forgive a person who had done grievous harm, the kind of harm that scraped channels in the stone of the brain. This kind of harm could not be remedied. It could not be made unharmful.

Was it forgiveness that Jennifer offered me? I do not know. I did not know then and I still do not know now. To think about being forgiven made me angry. It made my gut tighten and my head ache. It was a useless concept that had no practical application in the world, except to make people cry. Jennifer cried a lot while I was her carer, and she never hid her tears from me. A part of me was afraid of her tears, and afraid that she knew I was afraid, but she continued to cry and I had to bear witness.

I always thought that forgiveness was a kind of weakness. It meant letting someone harmful off the hook. It meant giving up on justice, something nobody should have to do when faced with an evil perpetrator. Eichmann.

To be forgiven for something terrible is what my mother would have called merciful. She would have quoted something to me from the Bible. There was a passage in Psalms about mercy that she was particularly fond of. Yes, I am sure my mother would have talked about mercy and redemption. She would have reminded me of the white swans and how they always point us towards the possibility of changing for the better. But I did not have the stomach for redemption or forgiveness or change. And now?

All I know is that I felt grateful to Jennifer, but not in the way I understood gratitude as a child. With Jennifer, it was a warm feeling, a good feeling, one that did not require me to behave in a certain way.

43

Five years passed, or the sun and the moon had tricked me. The professional carers continued to come to the house for the weekly bathe, and I was sent to my room for the duration of their visit.

This did not surprise me.

The small extra bone in my chest would become overactive shortly before their visit, a signal to prepare the bathroom and myself for their intrusion. I would carefully fold the dark blue towels and wipe the smears from the mirror. There were several bottles of lavender shampoo and bubble bath, which I lined up neatly along the edge of the bath. No detail was overlooked. The preparation became a quiet hour in the week, a time in which things became clearer to me, and my body relaxed.

Jennifer always made a point of thanking me profusely, as though she owed me something she could never repay.

Then one week, due to a staff shortage, the carers were unable to keep the appointment.

I cleaned the bathroom as usual, making sure to empty the bin and let in some fresh air. I wiped the tiles and even used a grout spray to scrub away the mould. I cleaned and polished the taps until they shone.

Downstairs, Jennifer was resting. I had helped her settle on her bed in the corner of the living room and she had asked me to leave the blind open. She did not want to sleep that afternoon, she had said. She would lie and listen to the clock instead. She seemed to be waiting for something.

I too stood still and waited. At some point, I thought the familiarity of waiting would comfort me, but it did not. I waited and waited. The bathroom was cleaner than it had ever been.

I went downstairs, but my footsteps were silent. When I moved, there was no sound. There was not even the stench of illness anymore. It was as though this world had become breathless, without air. I strained my ears to listen but there were no sounds at all, not even the clock. I went into the living room and took one step towards Jennifer's bed, but my movement made no sound. I opened my mouth and called to her, but my voice made no sound.

I stood beside her bed and sobbed.

44

On the bedside table was the small plate with dark blue flowers circling the rim, the one that I had given Jennifer all those years ago. I had always been especially careful in washing it, so that it remained intact.

The sound of a woman praying

45

Some things stay with you, whether they are true or not, whether they are valuable or not, and the story of preparing the body stayed with me.

I opened all the doors and windows in the downstairs of the house and went upstairs to run the bath. The bathroom was spotless and the afternoon sun was pouring in through the window. I could not stop crying, but when I stood still with my eyes closed facing directly into the sun, it was possible to see things – strange lights dancing on my eyelids – and to feel the intensity of the sun's power.

I left the bath running and went back downstairs to Jennifer. The air was cool and fresh, and the street outside was quiet.

I took the battery out of the bedside clock and turned it face down. In the hallway, I took my new coat off its peg and carefully hung it over the mirror.

I walked out into the back garden and stood in the spot where the pond had been. I did not know what to do. I did not think very much. All I knew was that I wanted to anoint her body and dress her in the red dress with the small white birds flying across the material in a repeat pattern. She would have liked that, I was sure.

But when I went to check the water, the bath had barely filled an inch, even though the taps were running on full bore. I checked the plug, but it was firmly in place. It was as though the water were running backwards up into the taps and pipes, instead of out into the bath. I got down on my knees beside the bath and stared at the small amount of water that had gathered. My small extra bone tapped and ticked. I could not fail Jennifer in this one task.

If I turned the taps off and then back on, perhaps they would right themselves. The room was beginning to get hot from the afternoon sun, which was blazing in through the windows. I opened them wide and took a deep breath. I did not know how long I could leave Jennifer alone before something went wrong. I did not know what that meant, only that I was feeling unsure and anxious in those moments after her death. What happens to the body in those first minutes and hours after death? How quickly did I need to act? I did not want to think about these things.

I could not stop crying, even as I turned the taps on and off, off and on; even as I walked upstairs and downstairs; even as I silenced the clock.

This day was not my choice and yet I had known long ago that it would come.

After what seemed like hours, I realised I would have to fill the bath with water from the kettle. It would take a very long time, but it did not matter. I could walk up and downstairs carrying the hot red kettle until there was enough bathwater to wash her body in. I must have walked a mile or two to fill that bath. The kettle must have boiled twenty times and every time I reset it to boil, I would stand and wait the five years it took to reach temperature.

A part of me was expecting to hear Jennifer call from the living room. I could not call it that anymore.

I put lavender bubble bath in the water and swished it around until it foamed. I added extra lavender oil because I knew this was Jennifer's favourite scent, and I did not find it unpleasant.

I had not said sorry to her. I was a fool, an imbecile, who took so very long to learn anything. It took me several years to accept this fact alone.

When the bath was finally ready, I returned to Jennifer and lifted her body into my arms. She was so light in those final weeks, it was like lifting a small bird. I carried her into the hallway and just as I was about to take her upstairs, Farah passed the wide-open front door. For one terrible moment, our eyes met. There was a darkness and a hatred in his eyes that would not abate. I could feel the hatred travel from him to me. It was as though the intensity of his hate became manifest in a palpable energetic form. It was dark blue, almost black.

I pushed the front door shut with my foot and carried Jennifer upstairs to the bathroom. I undressed her in silence. The sunlight seemed to dress her all over again.

I often wondered whether Jennifer had been aware of Farah's vile intentions towards me. She had never talked to me about it, but perhaps she had chosen to give him the benefit of the doubt. Shortly after I was released from prison and delivered to Jennifer's house, it was clear to me that Farah was watching my every move, waiting for just such an occasion to indict me. I knew he would never believe that Jennifer and I had become friends, and after the drowning of his dog, his determination to see me punished grew.

Had we been friends, Jennifer and I? I like to believe that we were in the end, that what I experienced in her company was real friendship. I felt safe with her. I no longer felt judged.

Her body was emaciated and done. A termination of doing and deeds and done.

I combed her hair carefully to remove any knots. It was thin and shoulder length and already knew about death.

Her whole body would not fit the length of the bath, and I had not thought about this. It was not easy washing and holding her gracefully, but I persevered. More than anything else, it was her fingers that moved me. I do not know why. Perhaps because they were so small and slender. The fragility of her body could not be overlooked; that years of illness had ravaged it, was evident. This was not a body of strength and nourishment, and yet Jennifer was the strongest person I had known.

I was careful in washing her, so that she remained intact. I did not want to harm any part of her, or accidentally damage her skin or stiffening limbs.

I gently rubbed her body with the lavender foam and oil. For me, it was a kind of anointment; a way of sending her off; a way of thanking her. The warm water masked the coolness of her flesh, and I was glad.

I had not said sorry to her.

I looked at her shrivelled breasts and remembered how she had laughed and teased her eroding body.

There was too much silence in the room.

46

It is not easy to live fully, but I believe Jennifer did. Even though her body succumbed to a terrible illness and she was wheelchair bound, I saw how fully she lived. I cannot describe what I mean and perhaps it does not matter. She did her best to be honest, something I have struggled with my whole life.

When I pushed her wheelchair back down Farah's drive, the evening we had taken him a consolatory meal, she had turned to me and said, 'It's not your fault, Quinn,' and the small extra bone in my chest seemed to stab my heart repeatedly. I had thought I was having a heart attack, but by the time we reached Jennifer's front door, the stabbing had stopped. I knew the drowning of Farah's dog was not my fault, but those words touched me deeply.

And I knew that Farah did not live fully. Like many people I have met, he pretended that his life was good and full, that he was a reliable and upstanding citizen. Perhaps I could see so clearly through this because of my own struggle? In any case, it did not surprise me that Farah took revenge, even though I had not wronged him.

47

I took Jennifer out of the bath with the utmost care. I laid her small body on a dark blue towel and wrapped her up in it. On the window, a spider was weaving a huge web, and the sun was catching the silk. She would have noticed this and smiled.

I moved a strand of her wet hair away from her face. I did not kiss her, but now I wish that I had.

This slow hour after Jennifer's death has stayed with me. I return to it again and again in my mind, even now.

Downstairs, I rummaged for her red dress with the small white birds flying across the material in a repeat pattern. Then I walked out into the hallway to find Martin standing there in his dark blue uniform with the name tag that read 'M. Payne'.

PART III

48

I do not know why, but in the immediate days follow-
ing Jennifer's death and my arrest – as a result of Farah's
trumped-up accusations of gross negligence – I felt what
I can only describe as a longing for my father. I do not
know why I thought of my father – his features, his gravelly
voice and mannerisms – I scarcely remember the man and
yet I felt this hunger in me to see and be with him then.
Perhaps it was an ache or loss of some kind, although I
was so familiar with those deprivations by then, that it
must surely have been something else. It was a feeling that
I could not explain.

During the long hours of waiting to find out my fate, the
father I barely remembered came back to my mind as a human
being, a man. Not like Stone Man – clearer, more honest. I
could see the way he used to tilt his head to the side when
he looked at my mother, the wry curl of the lip. I saw the
way he unscrewed the bottle or lifted the glass to his mouth.

I saw the small red flecks appearing like bright stars on my mother's pale cheeks. Who belonged there in that house?

The days and nights lengthened. It is not a lie to say that I was bewildered in a way I had never been before. It is not a lie to say that I grieved for Jennifer. And perhaps it is also true to say that I grieved for myself. I was in a kind of holding chamber, somewhere they kept people they did not know what to do with. It was small and dark, not unlike my old cell, except it was smaller and darker. There was no slit and the electric light was only switched on for a certain number of hours each day. If truth be told, I preferred lying in the dark to being accosted by the almost fluorescent strip light.

I had no idea how long I was there. Time became immeasurable, just as it had during my years in confinement, when there was no way of marking one day from the next. I did not know whether that was a good thing or not, but discerning fact from delirious fiction – trying to use a true winnowing fan – sometimes helped me in these hours and weeks and months of need: I knew that nothing lasted forever.

Nevertheless, I was going down. I mean that in all the ways that it can be understood. I would not have wanted to admit that I was a man on the brink of despair, but that is what I was. I thought my long years of experiencing the pain of incarceration would stand me in good stead for whatever might be thrown at me. But I was wrong.

49

I was going down and nothing and nobody could stop me.

Even now, I can picture Farah's face in court, his false testimony, his adamant righteousness. He repeatedly accused me of drowning his dog, as though this was proof enough to convict me of the gross negligence of Jennifer – the one person in the world who had given me a chance, a reprieve of sorts. But I was not a human being in Farah's eyes. I never had been, and I never would be.

It was the only time in court that I heard a judge momentarily silence the witness. Farah was told in no uncertain terms that he was to give a relevant eyewitness account that related to the charge he had levelled against me.

He told a series of convoluted and carefully considered lies. He lied from beginning to end, and there was neither physical evidence to support his testament nor corroborating statements from the professional carers. But how do you convince people of the truth when the lie is more comfortable, more acceptable to the fearful mind? When a man has already been convicted of a violent crime, how is it possible to regain the trust of those who stand in judgement of him a second time? It has taken decades for the truth of these questions to land in me. They are rhetorical, of course, and obvious to every thinking person. In all honesty, it is only now – well into my middle years – that I am beginning to learn how to think.

In the end, Farah's story of his dead dog proved enough to sow the seeds of disquiet and mistrust in the minds and hearts of the jury. He was a bitter, venomous man who knew how to manipulate the thoughts of others. He would have made a good journalist.

50

I did not like to think what they had done to her. I had left her small body wrapped in the dark blue towel on the floor in the bathroom. The bathwater would have gone cold and the foam would have dissolved. Perhaps there would still be the scent of lavender on the air or perhaps now there would be the stench of death.

I know now that what I felt for Jennifer was love. I know because there was a softness in me that was not there before. My father would have called this 'being soppy', but he was wrong − it was not a sentimental feeling, but a vulnerable one. There was something about Jennifer that softened me. I have no idea what it was.

I remember holding her red dress with the small white birds flying across the material in a repeat pattern. I remember Martin asking me what I was doing, and I put the dress down carefully over the banister as though I would shortly be taking it upstairs. The front door stood open behind Martin, and I could see the shadowy figure of Farah at the end of the path that led to Jennifer's door. He was hunched over like an old, arthritic man, with little life left in him. But I knew otherwise. I knew the power of this man's enmity, and when I glanced at him, I could feel the intensity of his loathing travel from his body towards mine. It was as though his hatred became manifest in a palpable energetic form. It was dark blue, almost black.

The afternoon was sunny but Farah's presence seemed to drain the sky of light. He was darker than the shadows cast by the box hedge and it felt like he was grinning, even though I could not see his face.

Martin repeated the question, but I do not remember answering. I wanted to stop him from going upstairs, not because I had anything to hide – on the contrary – but because I wanted to protect Jennifer. Once the backup officer arrived, Martin must have gone upstairs and found her body, though I have no memory of letting him pass.

He would not let me go into any of the rooms before we left. He would not let me see Jennifer one last time, and so I never had the chance to tell her how sorry I was. I knew that they would take her to the hospital for tests and place her body in the morgue. I know she would have told me that it was not my fault.

I held on to this knowing for as long as I could.

'Get your coat, Quinn. It's time to go.'

I picked up the new red coat that Jennifer had bought me, but Martin said he did not believe it was mine, and I was to get the coat I had arrived in. The fabric was too coarse for a coat. It was like rough, hairy skin and whenever the rain beat down, it became slippery.

I had wanted to make Jennifer's bed and straighten the blanket on her wheelchair. I had wanted to wipe down the old pine table and clean the crumbs out of the splits and knots. I had wanted to walk again in the garden where the pond used to be, and to stand at the fence line and look out across the fields where the foundations of a new housing estate had been abandoned. I had wanted to boil the bright red kettle one last time.

Martin escorted me out of the house in which I had begun to live as a man. He led me down the path towards Farah's hunched figure.

'Got any new stories, Quinn?' he hissed through his brown-yellow smoker's teeth.

Martin said nothing. I had to rub my hands together to remind myself that I had a body. It was a living body, for which I could be grateful. The small extra bone in my chest tapped and ticked, and tears began to run down my face, something I did not want either Farah or Martin to see.

Things have been done that hurt the mouth to speak of.

51

Four grey concrete walls, bed, desk, chair, bucket, slit.

It was not unusual for me to kill spiders, but I did not move. Instead, I watched it begin to weave a web in the corner of the slit. I did not understand immediately why it would weave its home there, when the wind and rain would batter it and make it less hospitable. It was a grey spider with darker grey markings and brown flecks. I did not know what kind it was. The spider was brighter and more courageous than I. It knew that in order to survive, it must take risks. Spider silk is stronger than human understanding.

Martin came to deliver a large envelope. It did not smell of lavender and I did not put it on the desk for later. I have learnt some things after all.

'Don't get your hopes up, Quinn. You've burnt your bridges now.'

But it was not true, since I never had a bridge in the first place; at least, not the kind that would withstand the fearful weight of others' ignorance. It was with sadness that I realised how easily someone like Martin could be duped, and that in this wounding grew a malicious cynicism. I only knew this well because of my own unravelling. I had liked Martin and respected him.

Farah, of course, was different. It felt as though he was unreachable through the veil of hatred that surrounded him. This veil was a kind of shield, since it allowed him to be certain about everything and protected him from the discomfort of hope. There was nothing comfortable about hope, but it was crucial. Spiders knew that.

The large envelope had been opened and resealed sloppily. Martin or some other prison officer would have checked the contents before giving it to me. It was bulky and oddly shaped, and it had my name written on it in block capitals. I immediately recognised the handwriting. Once Martin had gone, I sat on the bed and opened it.

Inside was a single swan feather from my mother.

52

It is true that most items are disallowed and confiscated, and so I was surprised that Martin let me keep the feather. Still, I did not believe it was a long-term favour and I worried that it might be used as a bargaining tool or a forfeit.

The feather was big enough to reach from my elbow to the tips of my fingers. It was whiter than anything I had seen for a long time. This size of feather must have come from a swan's wing. Jennifer would have liked this feather, and it would have been a good talisman to bury with her. Wings, after all, denote freedom.

The swans had inhabited the lake in the park, as though they were the only birds that truly mattered. They were haughty, I suppose, but also tranquil and strong. I could rely on them for those eternal characteristics. I liked them for that. Their presence in my life seemed to be an essential part of my learning. It was no wonder, therefore, that they showed up repeatedly: I was a very slow learner in the end.

What is there to say about my mother?

53

It was my mother's gift of the swan feather that later precipitated the hallucinatory dreams of our street and of Andrea.

I did not feel happy that she had contacted me in this way. She had not even bothered to write me a letter or a brief note. She had the audacity – after all these years – to send me something she knew would affect me greatly, but without words of love or even a simple greeting. For her, it was enough to scrawl my name on an envelope. For her, this kind of silence was a moral imperative, a way for her to neither condone nor console. She was able to keep herself clean by refusing to commit to either stance. What was more perfect to communicate such purity of heart than the gift of a swan's wing feather?

It was just as well she had not written. A part of me would have felt compelled to write back and I was afraid that things would be said that could not be unsaid. Words cannot be taken back. I was afraid that the old memories would crush me forever. It was better this way.

I wanted the swan's wing feather so badly and I did not want it at all. But I could not erase my mother, even though she had all but erased me.

5 4

The old familiar weariness and hunger were creeping back in and the small extra bone is my chest tapped and ticked. If it had not been for the whiteness of the feather, I might not have lasted long. Loneliness and sadness can kill a man, but I did not want pity.

I am a complicated man. I am an uncomplicated man. It is not for me to say how I have arrived at this paradox; not because I do not wish to speak of it – I do and I will – but because it is almost impossible to speak objectively about myself or the events of my life. All of us do it nonetheless. But the truth will hover somewhere between the words and the feelings they conjure.

55

It was a long, slow fall, but after all, I had the time.

It must have been winter because the cell was particularly cold and there was almost no daylight coming in through the slit. The hours of darkness were long and intense. Day was almost indistinguishable from night. At some point, I felt as if I were no longer in my body, even though I could still feel the coarseness of my strange coat wrapped around me.

During those long days or months of darkness, the cell changed. Nothing was straightforward anymore and I could not easily make out the bucket, desk, chair or even the slit. I remained on my bed, a pitiful, insect-like man with no purpose. I wanted to die. It was the second time in my life that I had truly wished for death to come. It was not out of self-pity, rather it was because the pain of being alive was too great. Perhaps that is the same thing? I do not know.

56

It was as though my ancestors had passed suffering on as a gift. A gift in dark blue, almost black wrapping paper that smelt of tar. I had never believed that suffering could migrate from one life to another across decades or even centuries. I never believed it, but it was true.

In those lonely days – a time that seemed eternal but passed like everything else – I dreamt that the walls of my cell became the dark concrete blocks of the housing estate where I lived as a child, the housing estate that was also home to Jennifer, Andrea and Farah. It was not an identical landscape – nothing ever is identical – but I was transported to a place that was familiar and also entirely alien to me.

The dreams were dark and they stayed with me in my waking hours. It seemed as though these were dreams my father could have dreamt, and his father and grandfather and great grandfather. It did not feel like they belonged only to me.

There was a shadowy street, where homeless people were begging along the entire length of the road; at least, I assumed they were homeless. They had dirty faces and missing teeth. Some of them wore rags and some of them wore clean white trainers. They did not seem to speak but made strange noises that sounded like animals in pain. It was a kind of high-pitched screaming that made my head ache.

The street was sticky. As I walked along, I realised that the surface of the road had melted and the tar was oozing and cloying to my boots. It was very difficult to pull my legs up one at a time, to take a step and then another. I had to use all my powers of concentration and patience to be able to walk, to employ a basic motor skill that had been effortless my whole life. The tar smelt strong. There was no way to side-step it, since there was no verge or pavement. The beggars were sitting or squatting down on the road, but the patches of tar where they were had not melted and their trainers – those who had them – were still blazing white and free of the black goo.

Around me I could hear the high-pitched screaming of the beggars and in the brief lulls between their voices, the squawking of crows. There were three crows sitting on the roof of the house next door to Jennifer's – not Farah's house, but the one on the other side. I had never met the people who lived there and when I looked more closely at the house, it seemed uninhabited; at least, the curtains were all closed and the front garden was overgrown and ugly.

When I turned back to the road, the tar had solidified with

my feet buried in it. I could not move and there was a figure standing in front of me, a small boy with a moth where his face should have been. Instead of the usual human features, he had the unmistakable wings of an emperor moth, slowly opening and closing, like a mouth opens and closes as it speaks. The small, furry body of the moth was positioned on the central line of his face, with the moth's black bead eyes at the top, where his forehead would have been. When he spoke, his voice seemed to come from somewhere in his chest.

'Watch!' he said, and so I watched as he walked over to the house where the crows were, whistled them down off the roof and proceeded, one by one, to cut out their tongues.

I do not know why this affected me so deeply. I stood, glued into the road, sobbing and wailing as the boy mutilated the birds. I never cared for crows, but there was something about this act and the startling moth face of the boy that broke my heart.

'Please, stop!' I beseeched, but he did not.

After what felt like days, even weeks, the moth boy came over to me and cut my feet free from the tar. As I stepped out and put my bare feet down on the solid surface of the road, I noticed that the wailing of the beggars had stopped. I wanted to reprimand the boy for what he had done to the crows, but I could not speak.

'Come on,' he said, and pulled me by the arm further down the road.

57

I did not want to go to my parents' house, but the boy was strong and he pulled me forwards, no matter how much I resisted. Their house was the last but one on the street, before the road turned into woodland, the place where Andrea and I played as children.

The house was almost as I remembered it. The front door had the same frosted-glass panel in the shape of a teardrop. The dark blue, almost black gloss paint was still peeling off the window frames. The only difference was the garden: it had become an overgrown tangle of briars and weeds, which would have horrified my mother.

There was nobody there and I was glad. I turned away from the house to go, but the boy pointed to the back garden and began dragging me with him around the side of the house. The moth was flapping its wings wildly, as though it was trying to take off. I could see the moth's small, furry body pulsing with energy, and it nauseated me.

The back garden was just as overgrown and the rose bushes that my mother had planted had been taken over by honeysuckle and bindweed. All the plants had lost their colour, and even the grass was a kind of grey mush beneath my bare feet.

In the far corner of the garden, a lone swan had built a nest. The boy pointed at the bird and nodded his head. I was to go over to it. It was a stupid place for a swan to nest, given there was no pond or river nearby. The bird had dragged all kinds of grass, sticks and undergrowth into an impressive nest beneath the laburnum, and inside the nest was an enormous egg. The white of her body was startling against the grey drabness of the garden.

As soon as I got within an arm's length of her, she attacked.

58

My body ached where the blows had come. My lower back was immovable. I lay still for many days – any movement triggered pain – so still, in fact, that Martin came in to check that I was still alive. There was shallow breathing somewhere in me.

My face was bleeding. There was one particularly painful wound just beneath my right eye. I could tell that it was quite deep, that I could have put the tip of my little finger inside it and felt the wetness. A throbbing, stinging pain, and that vulnerable, gashed feeling that comes when a wound is open to the air.

59

I began a letter to my mother. I had neither pen nor paper, and I did not even know where she lived. Perhaps Martin would have brought me what I needed, but I did not ask him for help. Instead, I composed the letter in my mind. I began it a thousand times and tore it up a thousand times. I did not know what to say to her. I did not know how to begin, but I also did not know how to end. In spite of everything, there was something in me that wanted to contact her, to be in her presence, to hear her voice.

Dear Mama.

No, I would not begin like that. She was not dear to me.

I prepared a long list of questions for her, as though there would eventually come a time when she and I would sit together and talk about our lives. I do not know why I clung to this idea – it was ridiculous! Even if I was released within the next decade, she would be old by then, and frail. She never was one for engaging in frank conversation – unless it related to the Bible – and so I could not imagine her to be willing in her old age either, quite the opposite in fact. Why should she soil the last years of her life with the truth, that dark blue, almost black story that had been silenced for so long?

It was her choice to submerge the story, to hold it beneath the waves until it drowned. The tragedy, of course, was her ignorance or wilful blindness: some stories are anaerobic and take place in total darkness, somewhere deep and hidden. Not all stories require oxygen to survive.

In reality, the questions were a waste of time, but I posed them anyway. In my imaginary conversations, anything was possible: my mother could make us tea and cake, and pull up two chairs to a brightly lit table; she could wrap a warm blanket around my shoulders; she could extend a hand to my arm or even kiss my cheek; she could listen.

Yours faithfully. Yours truly. As ever.

60

I fell in love with Andrea the day she pointed out the Himalayan poppy to me – the year she and Jennifer moved into our street. I fell in love with her because she also liked ponies and birds of all kinds. She was, even in those very early days, my dear white swan. She taught me everything I know about flowers and trees, their names and when they bloomed and which ones only bloomed once. Of course, I have forgotten the names of most things and can barely remember what the keys of the ash tree look like or where the bluebells grow. This is not surprising since I have been locked away now for longer than I have been free – if that is what we can call it. I know the different shades of grey concrete very well and I can guess the time of day by the way the sun slants across the desk. I can still recognise the cawing of a crow, the twittering trill of a swallow and the *tchack* of a jackdaw, but most of the outside world has been taken away from me. It is a hard punishment, the magnitude of which I had not expected.

It is only now that I see why the story I had written of the swan would have bored her. Some part of her believed in the purity of the heart, something greater than her that she had to fight for every day, especially after her mother became ill. She was not interested in the swan's manipulation or control. In fact, she actively chose to embrace the opposite – a kind of surrender to whatever her life presented her with. She was not a saint, but she knew how to love.

She was everything my mother was not.

61

Every night for what must have been several weeks, Andrea appeared to me in my dreams.

I do not know how to speak of this. I do not know how to be trusted with words anymore. What does a true word look like in any case? I do not know who will believe me or who will score me out, and so I have to speak into a void and hope that at least someone might listen.

The darkness that engulfed me after Jennifer's death was a different kind of suffering to the one I experienced after my first sentencing – after I was convicted of Andrea's killing. It is beyond painful to speak these words aloud. My body rebels against them, but these are what true words look like after all.

Perhaps this is the reckoning that Jennifer spoke of.

62

It was the love of these two women that taught me how to kneel, even though I was a slow learner. There was to be no altar, no religious paraphernalia of any kind; there was to be only Quinn kneeling before his own bloody truth.

It was an agony beyond words.

63

To begin with, the dreams of Andrea were vague. That is to say, I did not picture her as she was in life, but as an indistinct form standing beneath the slit in my cell, a plump, shadowy figure emitting soft white light. She was a black and white photograph of movement, where the eye constantly shifts to find focus and meaning. But I knew it was her. I would drift in and out of sleep towards dusk, as the light was fading from the cell and the slit was taking the last rays back out into the sky. Early in the evening, as the spider's web ceased to catch the light, I knew she would soon visit me in my dreams.

I did not welcome these visitations.

I no longer knew who I was and the pain in my lower back was almost unbearable. I could not stop thinking about Jennifer, and yet thinking about her and the time I had spent as her carer was too painful to dwell on. It made the reality of the cell intolerable. Inside my head, one thousand maggots chewed incessantly at my brain. I would not have been surprised to wake one morning to find the flesh of my scalp and face consumed. Sometimes the pain was so acute, I took to convincing myself that my time with Jennifer had never taken place. It was easier that way.

Inside the pocket of my strange coat was the small plastic figurine that Andrea had given me and the small white duck feather from the pond that never was. I held them in one palm and could not forget so readily.

There was something new about this suffering, something I can only describe as a kind of bloodletting. I do not know what that means, except that there was a sense of being emptied, excavated, sucked clean.

64

During the first series of dreams, Andrea appeared but did not speak. The quality of her presence reminded me of a moment in her garden, not long after we had first met. My mother and Jennifer were chatting on the lawn and Andrea was staring at a flower; we must have been about five or six years old.

'Look at this, Tomek,' she said and pointed out the Himalayan poppy that was bursting with colour, an almost surreal blue in her mother's herbaceous border. There was just one flower and the stem was slightly hairy, like all poppy stems, and pale green, the colour of tranquillity. The petals did not seem real to me. I could not understand how something could be so beautiful and so fragile at the same time. I looked at them and wanted to touch, to pull at the petals to see if they were real. 'No!' she said. 'Be careful! They're soft. You have to be kind to them, Tomek.' And I said to her, 'My name is Quinn.'

She did not call me Tomek again, even though she heard my mother calling me this nickname. She saw that I liked to be called Quinn, our surname, and she honoured that. She knew how to respect small things.

It was my father who had begun calling me Quinn, as though I was a boy in the army or a man in prison. To be known by one's surname had a certain manliness to it, or so I thought. It made me feel important, different to the other members of my family and different to my friends. Besides, everybody knows that Tomek is a name for a crying boy.

Being addressed by one's surname is not manly, of course. It is not honourable. In fact, it is quite the opposite. I have delighted in calling Balram Farah by his surname all these years. He will always be Farah to me, as though he too is a faceless man in prison. He does not deserve my respect. Besides, his name is a lie: his forename, 'Balram', means 'a brother of Krishna' and his surname, 'Farah', means 'joy'.

Andrea's presence in my dreams was both a comfort and a threat. She wanted something from me and I did not know how to give it. I was still a fool and she knew it. She had a sixth sense, I think, a kind of knowing that some women have. It was as though she saw the very insides of me. I do not mean the blood and sinew and bone, rather the intention and judgement and fear. To her, these things were garments worn by the person with more or less aplomb. A hat of fear. A vest of intention. A scarf of judgement. She would often tell me about myself as though from the inside out, as though she were not separate from me at all.

She saw the shadow in me, the hidden darkness that wanted to claim me for its own, and she loved me all the same. She was just like the Himalayan poppy.

The sound of a woman praying

65

In the dreams, Andrea would stand beneath the slit and scrutinise me as the day turned to night. My dream self did not approach her or try to touch her. Something in me knew that I was to be still and wait, although I did not know what I was waiting for.

In the days and nights that followed, it felt as though the dreams were more real than my waking life. They were so lifelike and visceral that I became afraid. Was I hallucinating? Was my mind deceiving me?

As the dreams became more vivid, Andrea's form became more clearly defined, until the shape of her stood intact and absolute in the cell. She had the body of a white swan and the head of a woman, her own head with those dark blue eyes and thin, shoulder-length golden hair. It was not appealing to me. In fact, there was something ugly and unpleasant about this combination, particularly because her feathers and face were so white and her eyes so dark. She did not look compliant.

When she stretched out her wings, they engulfed the whole cell. They were certainly bigger than I was, something that no longer surprised me. My body had diminished, while hers had grown in splendour, or if not splendour, then power.

She did not speak out loud to me, but her voice was in my head like a siren. I was instructed to climb onto her back as in the tales of old – I was not offered a choice – so that she could take me to some far-off place. It was not uncomfortable in the folds of her feathers. She was so enormous and strong that I felt like a child or a skeleton of my former self, wrapped in the arms of a mighty benevolence. I had never felt more awake nor more held, but a part of me was afraid: the part that knew where she was taking me.

We flew for a long time. It was neither real nor dreamlike. Five years passed, or the sun and the moon had tricked me, and I had no memory of our landing.

The woods were darker than I remembered and dense. Daylight had not yet fully penetrated the crisscross of branches and the place felt inert, more plantation than woodland. We must have flown all night. Birds were calling – tits, wood pigeons – and everything was wet from recent rain. Andrea and I were alongside each other beneath the trees. She moved forwards on her big webbed feet and

I followed. Mud and leaves reluctantly let go of my boots. There was nothing erotic about it.

I had never understood about mud or reluctance or rain.

We headed straight for the silver birch, our tree. The sun was beginning to shine between clouds, and the bark glowed. One white incisor in a forest of teeth – that's what Andrea called it. She was standing with her wings close to her body and her long neck stretched up towards the lower branches of the birch tree. This was the place we met on Fridays, after she had finished with Jennifer and I had completed the week's story. A single silver birch in the middle of larch and pine, and the big car-wash brushes of spruce.

My body began to ache and my lower back became so painful I had to crouch down and then lie flat on the woodland floor. I lay moaning for some time, and Andrea watched me without speaking. She did not offer me solace of any kind and I knew that this was as it should be. My body was breaking by my own hand.

I lay helpless and Andrea stood above me with her powerful, feathered body beside the silver birch. Slowly at first, she began to bleed. Dark red droplets appeared on the woodland floor, pooling at her feet and then rapidly becoming a torrent of woman blood. At least, I thought it was her blood. Inside the fear and strangeness of the dream, I thought *she* was the open wound, whereas in fact the blood was mine. I was losing everything.

In no time the blood rose to reach the white feathers of her swan body. The untainted surface was spoilt. I did not want to watch, but my eyes were forced open by her demands: I was to look. I was to watch how the blood travelled from my body out into the woodland. I was to observe how the blood gathered, to notice how thick blood can be and how it can amass in sticky globs inside the tiny concave forms of dead leaves.

The blood rose up across the woodland floor so that I was soon lying in a sea of blood, viscous and warm. I did not want to drown in my own blood, but I could neither speak nor move and the level was rising.

Andrea watched me struggle, her face pale and implacable. As the blood rose, she demanded I move nearer the birch tree and get up on all fours. Her swan body was at home on the lake of blood, and she paddled gracefully in circles around me.

I was like a dog at the foot of a tree, Farah's lame dog, who could neither run away nor swim. I had to hold my head upright in order not to drown.

This was the place that used to be *our* place. This was where Andrea and I met on Fridays after she had finished with her mother and I had completed the week's story. I remembered everything.

66

Each evening at dusk, for a further nine consecutive evenings, the same dream journey was undertaken, and each time it was as if for the first time. I had to experience everything anew, over and over. It was only briefly during waking hours that I was aware of the repetition of the dream, and I became afraid that this was my life now, that I would have to endure this bloody horror every night for the rest of my time in prison.

I was not a plausible man. I was a plausible man.

I spent many hours of the day holding Andrea's small plastic figurine in my hand, to study its features and to wait; I thought the doll could speak to me or had something to offer that could console me. But it was an illusion.

It was during those days that I suffered the most. The weariness and the hunger came into my body like a cancer, saturating my living cells with their dark blue, almost black disease. There were times when I was not in my body – the pain in my torso and limbs was too much to bear. My hands hung like dead fish. Slowly, over the course of those days, the details of my life began to crystallise, and I saw, perhaps for the first time, what I had done.

It was not that Martin came and told me the story that I had forgotten. The memories came back of their own accord, piecemeal at first, and then they flooded back in a tide that was stronger than I had thought possible. The swan feather that my mother had sent would not let me forget or turn away from my deeds.

It was my own hands that had done wrong; hands that had been made by my mother and my father; hands that had stroked the forehead of my brother as he lay dying; and hands that had hit the walls of my room until the knuckles bled. These hands had patted the flanks of ponies, learnt how to cut fresh bread, how to write with a pen, how to turn on a tap and turn it off again. These hands with lifelines that show the way to go or the way that has been or the way that is yet to come. These hands that wanted so badly to hold and never let go, but which misunderstood everything. These hands had thought they knew how to love. These hands, even when they were young, had wanted to tear the poppy, to pull it apart to make sure it was real.

I was a plausible man. I was not a plausible man.

67

It is true that Andrea was the one person in the world I trusted.

Her death was my fault. I should have been more aware. *Mistaka.* In error, I took everything from her, and almost everything from myself.

It is true that there is no way to excuse what I did. I will have to repeat this sentence over and over for the rest of my life, not because I need to remind myself, but because it is probably the only way for others to make room for me on this earth.

68

I tried to bring Andrea back, but her body was lifeless.

I vomited into the bushes near where we had lain. To this day, I remember the stench of it, the acrid gall.

It was the first time in my life that I had wanted to die. The pain of my life was nothing compared to this. Sometimes, I wish I had hung myself there and then.

Five years passed, or the sun and the moon had tricked me. It was as though I was in a parallel world. I sobbed helplessly.

69

I do not remember all the small details. I remember all the small details.

They say that they found her body, but they have not. They say that they found her body, and that is true in a worldly sense, I know, but in my heart the living body of Andrea abides.

There is nothing I can say to make this better. It is at this point that words fall into an abyss, like the horse running at full tilt across the page. Except I am not running; I am forced to sit still and face this dark truth.

70

The last time I dreamt of Andrea, she did not take me to the woods. She stood resolute beneath the slit and spoke to me. Her body glowed. She stretched out her long swan neck, so that her face loomed close to mine.

'What have you done, Quinn? What have you done?' These words came out in a hiss, pressing onto my eyeballs. 'It's pointless to ask a man this question when he doesn't even know who he is. You don't know who you are! For all your years, Quinn, for all your learning, you still don't know who you are!'

Her dark blue eyes bore into me and I could feel the cold clamminess of her presence on my skin. In the dream, she was as powerful as she had been in life, and my broken body shook and shrank. In that moment, I remembered Jennifer's red dress, the one with small white birds flying across the material in a repeat pattern.

Her body had grown so big it almost filled the cell, pushing into all four corners, concealing the door and the slit. I was forced up against the concrete wall and could see nothing but the white of her feathered body and the blazing white of her face, up close to mine. There was almost no breath in my body. She was so close to me and so all-encompassing, it felt as though my own body had disappeared.

'When you walk in the woods, Quinn, as in future years you will, you'll remember what you've done and you'll kneel.'

Her words came into me like cut-glass vases. There was nothing to say in reply and I knew she did not want or need me to speak. Words were no use anymore. I reached down into the pocket of my strange coat and my hand gripped the small plastic figurine that Andrea had once given to me. I held it up to her, tears of remorse and sadness pouring down my face. It was the only thing I had left to offer.

She took it in her furious mouth and swallowed the doll down.

71

I never saw Andrea again. She no longer visited me in my dreams. I like to think that both she and Jennifer are at peace now, but I do not know.

Five years passed, or the sun and the moon have tricked me. I often recall Farah's dog – her softness and ease that afternoon in the sunlight, the way she lay with her legs stretched fully out and her body in a slight curve. It was as though she knew about the shape of a new moon and was telling us that was who she was: the perfect slither, hanging clean in the world. I never knew her to be aggressive, except in defending herself from the drakes. She lay flat on the floor because she wanted to. It was for joy; she was still because joy was in it.

Things have been done that hurt the mouth to speak of. But I am speaking now.

Acknowledgements

This book has been a labour of love. It began in 2016 with a movement practice and the first line of the story. So many people have been part of this book and I want to give thanks here.

If I hadn't worked in Scottish prisons for a decade and if the men there hadn't shared their time with me, I wouldn't have had the courage to write this book. Thank you to all the incarcerated men I have worked with since 2013.

Thank you to Iranian writer, Sadegh Hedayat, whose spirit lives on. During the preliminary stages of writing, I visited his grave in Père Lachaise Cemetery, Paris, but that's another story.

Thank you to all my early readers and encouragers, especially Rach Connor, Iain Galbraith, Paul Kingsnorth, Jane Murray, Roger Bygott, Kath Burlinson, Nigel Hollidge, Frank Stack, Christine Sparks and my beloved husband, Dougie, whose kindness I couldn't live without.

Thank you, Jacques Testard, for seeing Quinn's potential and for leading Irene Baldoni to me. Thank you, Irene, for your brilliance – in all meanings of the word.

And finally, thank you, Juliet Mabey, for your patient and astute editorial eye. Thank goodness you nudged me when I needed nudging!